EDWARD THOMAS

Faber Student Guides

EDWARD
THOMAS

Stan Smith

faber and faber

LONDON · BOSTON

First published in 1986 by
Faber and Faber Limited
3 Queen Square London WC1N 3AU

Typesetting by
Goodfellow & Egan Ltd, Cambridge
Printed in Great Britain by
Redwood Burn Ltd Trowbridge Wiltshire

© Stan Smith 1986

British Library Cataloguing in Publication Data

Smith, Stan, 1943–
Edward Thomas: students' guide
1. Thomas, Edward, 1878–1917,
Criticism and interpretation
I. Title 821′.912   PR6039.H55Z/

ISBN 0-571-13942-6

Library of Congress Cataloging-in-Publication Data

Smith, Stan, 1943–
Edward Thomas.
(A Faber student guide)
Bibliography: p.
1. Thomas, Edward, 1878–1917—Criticism and interpretation.
I. Title.   II. Series.
PR6039.H55Z795 1986   821′.912   86-11544
ISBN 0-571-13942-6 (pbk.)

The Faber Student Guides

In an age when critical theory promises, or threatens, to 'cross over' into literature and to become its own object of study, there is a powerful case for re-asserting the primacy of the literary text. The Faber Student Guides are intended in the first instance to provide substantial critical introductions to writers of major importance. Although each contributor inevitably writes from a considered critical position, it is not the aim of the series to impose a uniformity of theoretical approach. Each Guide will make use of biographical material and each will conclude with a select bibliography which will in all cases take note of the latest developments usefully relevant to the subject. Beyond that, however, contributors have been chosen for their critical abilities as well as for their familiarity with the subject of their choice.

Although the primary aim of the series is to focus attention on individual writers, there will be exceptions. Among our future plans are studies of the fiction of the First and Second World Wars; and of Edwardian drama. And although the majority of writers or periods studied will be of the twentieth century, this is not intended to preclude other writers or periods – as the study of Emily Dickinson shows. Above all, the series aims to return readers to a sharpened awareness of those texts without which there would be no criticism.

John Lucas

In memory of Uncle Bill Flannery and 'Uncle' Tom Martin, both survivors of the Great War – the one Empire Loyalist and Irish nationalist, the other shop steward and ILP activist; the two, inseparable friends. From them I first learned the contradictoriness of 'England'. Of each it could be said: 'Everybody has met one such man as he'.

Contents

Acknowledgements

Many years ago, Helen Thomas was kind enough to put at my disposal for as long as I needed them several large volumes of her husband's reviews. These volumes are now deposited in the Edward Thomas Collection at the University of Cardiff. For her tremendous generosity and for the many kindnesses of her and her daughter Myfanwy, I would like to put my gratitude on record. I hope that this book in some ways justifies their trust. Equally long ago Professor Graham Hough was a kind and helpful supervisor of a thesis which he would no longer, I think, recognize in this, its remote lineal descendant. Earlier versions of some of the material here have appeared in the journals *Critical Quarterly, Literature and History, Poetry Review* and *Delta,* and I should like to thank their editors for their encouragement. I am grateful to the following libraries for their assistance: New York Public Library (Berg Collection), Dartmouth College Library, Lockwood Memorial Library, Buffalo, The British Library, National Library of Scotland, Cambridge University Library. John Lucas has been a considerate and thoughtful series editor, and I am indebted to him for many kindnesses, past and present. R. J. C. Watt, as ever, read and commented on the text. But as always my main debt for keeping me and this book going lies with Jennifer Birkett, an honour she now shares somewhat dubiously with an IBM PC, without whom none of it would have been possible. Needless to say, no one, not even the computer, is responsible for the views expressed here, except myself.

I

A Superfluous Man

Edward Thomas is the quintessential English poet. His poem 'Adlestrop' has graced countless anthologies as the definitive English idyll. His country books *The Heart of England* and *The South Country* have delineated authoritatively that area from Kent to Gloucestershire which, in the literary tradition, is the heart of Englishness. Many British critics have found in his work an alternative, native tradition to set against the cosmopolitan Modernism of Eliot, Yeats and Pound. Andrew Motion, for example, in *The Poetry of Edward Thomas* (1980, pp. 10-11), finds in his words, as in his blackbirds, 'an expression of stable Englishness'. In his Englishness, for Motion, Thomas links Hardy and other 'writers who were, to use his own words in "Lob", "English as this gate, these flowers, this mire"', with such subsequent 'colonizers of the fruitful middle ground' between modernity and tradition as W. H. Auden, R. S. Thomas, Philip Larkin and Ted Hughes – poets who have 'justified his evolutionary rather than revolutionary aims'.

Yet this list of 'English' poets is subtly disturbed by the presence in their midst of Edward Thomas's namesake, R. S. Thomas who, though certainly an *Anglican* clergyman, is no less certainly a *Welsh* poet. That Motion seems to include Robert Frost, who in 1914 persuaded Thomas to take up writing poetry and whose *North of Boston* provided his model, almost as an honorary Englishman in this 'evolutionary' alternative to Modernism likewise adds a certain slipperiness to the idea of Englishness. Thomas did not make the same mistake about Frost, finding in the added tang of Americanness of his diction and characters the clue by contrast to what was specifically English, as he wrote to John Freeman on 14 August 1914: 'It is curious to have such good natural English with just that shade of foreignness in the people and the poet himself. In some ways he seems as American as writers who use far more American words and turns and more particularly localized material.' For a poet as subtle in his discriminations as Thomas, such an observation is important.

When critics such as Motion speak of Thomas belonging to a 'fruitful middle ground', when they emphasize the continuity of Englishness, as one uninterrupted evolutionary process, they are celebrants at the ritual renewal of an ideological myth. That Thomas himself, in part at least, also participated in this myth, should not lead us to overlook a countervailing strand in his work. Thomas's heralding of Frost's volume as 'one of the most revolutionary books of modern times', poems which are 'revolutionary because they lack the exaggeration of rhetoric' (*Daily News*, 22 July 1914), is cited by Motion in discussing Thomas's Englishness, without any sense of how it actually contradicts that insistence on 'evolution'. Thomas is speaking primarily, of course, about a literary revolution. But one who had read 'a very illuminating paper' to the Davenant Society at Oxford on 'the wave of Revolution, the break-up of Europe and the threatened destruction of society, and the genesis of a new literature as exemplified in the poems of Coleridge and Wordsworth' (Cooke, p. 30) was well aware of the interdependence of literary and political moments.

[12]

There is, after all, one major complication to the concept of Thomas as *the* English poet: his Welshness. The great Welsh radical Prime Minister David Lloyd George wrote in the foreword to John Moore's *The Life and Letters of Edward Thomas* that 'I am interested and attracted by him and his work, firstly, because he was a Welshman'. On the centenary of his birth he was the object of a complete special issue of *Poetry Wales*. When Thomas celebrates the 'English words' of the poem 'Words', it is without surprise that he finds them at their most resonant in the speech of 'Wales, / Whose nightingales / Have no wings'. Besides his English country books Thomas also wrote *Beautiful Wales;* and ironically, as he himself was the first to point out, *The Heart of England* itself ends in Wales, while an imaginary castle calls up the Arthurian romances which precede any settled Englishness.

All of his life Thomas thought of himself as an expatriate Welshman. What he refers to as his 'accidentally Cockney nativity' in Lambeth on 3 March 1878 was the result of demographic shifts over which he had no control and for which he accepted no responsibility. His father, Philip Henry Thomas, had recently moved with his wife Mary Elizabeth from Tredegar to London, like many Welshmen, seeking work and social improvement. The continuing expansion of the railway system throughout the second half of the century had brought many such migrations for the people of South Wales, first from the countryside to the new urban centres and then, as the population growth caused by rapid industrialization produced a surplus of labour and skills, overflowing the valleys themselves to London and the English Midlands. By the last quarter of the century Wales was beginning to feel quite strongly the recession differentially afflicting the global economy.

Thomas's birth in rented rooms in what was primarily a lower-class district testifies to the comparative poverty in which his parents initially found themselves. His father's job as a staff clerk for light railways at the Board of Trade soon brought a definite move up in the world. When the young Philip Edward was two, a second child was expected, and the family moved to a larger house of their own in Wandsworth. When he was ten the family (now with five sons) moved again several streets away to a large detached house in what still seemed the semi-rural suburb of Clapham, with its common, like Wandsworth's, allowing the countryside to creep closer to the heart of the city. Here what was ultimately a family of six sons found itself affluent enough to hire a succession of occasional servants, many themselves of Welsh origin. These migrations were only lesser versions of a whole history of transplantings which give the lie to the myth of England as one people living perpetually in the same place.

Thomas's Welsh ancestors themselves derived from families who had crossed the Severn estuary from Somerset and Devon in an earlier period, as the survival of West Country names in the family records attests. Thomas himself adopted as a pseudonym for his first poetry publications the name of 'Edward Eastaway', one of the litany of ancestral names he celebrates in *The South Country,* speaking of the West calling 'with a voice of dead Townsends, Eastaways, Thomases, Phillipses, Treharnes, Marendaz, sea men and mountain men' (p. 8). Thomas's paternal grandfather, a fitter, had moved in turn from the rural hinterland of Caermarthenshire to Tredegar, in the Welsh iron and coal belt, where Thomas's father was born. He subsequently moved again to the Welsh ghettos of the railway town of Swindon in Wiltshire,

[14]

where he and his son Harry worked as fitters on the Great Western Railway. It was here that, visiting his widowed grandmother and uncle during his school-holidays, the young Thomas formed his strongest images of that landscape which he was to make his own.

The importance Thomas attached to his sense of his ancestry is intimately bound up with his fretting about deracination. That he could himself embrace his Welshness and yet at the same time not feel the strain of reconciling it with his idea of England testifies to the power of ideology to contain contradictions. Yet the strain is apparent everywhere in his work, focused most acutely in that sense of perpetual exile which pervades his poetry. Linked with this is the idea of 'accidence'.

Thomas wrote in 1900 to a Scottish friend who had been a fellow undergraduate at Oxford: 'After all Wales is good for me. In spite of my accidentally Cock-ney nativity, the air here seems to hold in some virtue essential to my well-being, and I always feel, in the profoundest sense, at home' (Moore, p. 277). In 1908, he used the word 'accidental' to describe the identity of the Welsh towns, in a way which unconsciously links with his own sense of being a flimsily rootless creature, whose own identity is a congeries of contradictory influences, in danger of a similar suburbanization of the spirit:

> The Welsh towns are either large villages ... or accidental mercantile and manufacturing congeries like Swansea and so far as I know the Welsh element in them is of no importance except to make for confusion and ugliness by its provincialism. The country is still rude and strong and full of goodness, but I do not see how it is to be shaped ... It is in danger of being a London suburb. It is a pity it has nothing to revolt for

[15]

> like Ireland . . . You may be able to help me to connect
> more definitely with Wales, with which I am flimsily
> connected now by birth, a few acquaintances, love of
> the country and a useless sentiment. (Moore, p. 306)

The tension here, between acquiescence in a double
dependency (surburbanized provincialism), and revolt
into autonomous identity (the Irish model), is one that
runs through Thomas's own life as a personal conflict.

The Happy-Go-Lucky Morgans is a fictionalized
narrative which draws heavily on Thomas's own suburban childhood, overlapping, at points, with the more
direct memories of his autobiographical fragment, *The
Childhood of Edward Thomas*. Both works emphasize
the important formative influence of the suburbs,
something which was to be a recurrent theme of
Thomas's prose for the rest of his life. At the same
time, both works contrast with this influence that of
'the wilderness', whether it is the secret gardens of
large empty houses nearby or the hidden places of
Wiltshire and Wales. In one episode in the novel we are
subjected to a patriotic sermon on England ('Mr
Stodham Speaks for England'), at which point fog
supervenes, one character ironically strikes up 'Rule
Britannia', and the narrator, remembering this scene
from his childhood, recalls that he was provoked to
respond: 'This raised my gorge; I could not help shout-
ing "Home Rule for Ireland".' Conflict seems to have
been rounded off into cosiness by a chorus of the Welsh
anthem 'Land of My Fathers' when the quietly subversive Aurelius inserts a new conflict, that of class,
into the proceedings. '"I really did not know before", he
remarks, "that England was not a shocking fiction of the
journalists and politicians . . . But what about the
London fog? What is the correct attitude of a patriot
towards London fog and the manufacturers who make it
what it is?"' The fog is not, after all, a fact of

nature, but a human artefact. Aurelius is suggesting that 'England' is not an unproblematic unity, but a complex and contradictory site. As the stresses and strains of Thomas's writings indicate, this site is criss-crossed by many, conflicting forces: class, culture, nationality, generation, gender, and what he himself called 'race'. For Mr Stodham to claim that 'The more you love and know England the more deeply you can love the Wilderness and Wales', is to repress the real and problematic complexity of 'England' into a convenient myth.

The argument of this book is that Thomas's biography enshrines a double story. In one sense, his life follows a simple trajectory. From the prosperous South London suburbs he becomes a day boy at prestigious middle-class schools, a 'free scholar' at Battersea Grammar School and then, from the age of sixteen, a pupil at St Paul's public school. His father wishes him to follow him into the civil service, but naturally enough he rebels against this, develops an interest in literature, and, at the age of sixteen, accidentally makes the acquaintance of the writer James Ashcroft Noble, whose patronage brings him the publication of his first book, a collection of nature writings, *The Woodland Life,* in 1897. It also brings him into contact with Noble's daughter, Helen. The two become close and, after her father's death, lovers. By the time Edward's father has decided to finance him to read for a History degree at Lincoln College, Oxford, the track is marked out. In his second year at Oxford, Helen becomes pregnant. It is an in-evitable accident, given their bohemian, feminist free thinking and their (unfortunate) naïvety about contra-ception. Under pressure from even their libertarian friends, they marry half secretly at Fulham Registry Office in June 1899.

Disappointed in his degree (a second), Thomas fails

on graduation in 1900 to get the college fellowship that would have saved him from genteel poverty. For the remaining years of his life he is to slave away as a literary hack, reviewing, writing potboilers, producing in the end nearly forty books, in order to sustain a growing family, moving through a succession of houses around London and the Downs. When the Great War breaks out (as the result of a monstrous accident at Sarajevo) it seems to offer Thomas the possibility of an escape from the miserable routine of marriage and endless unrewarding writing. He enlists in the Artists' Rifles in July 1915 and, at the age of 39, is killed by a stray shell at the battle of Arras on 9 April 1917. Almost by accident, one might say.

In the brief period between December 1914 and his death, his (accidental) encounter with Robert Frost, and the impetus of the war, have led him to produce a body of poetry which testifies for ever to his love of the English countryside and its people, flowers and animals. The cosy myth heals over into a celebration of that charmed Georgian peace broken for ever by the brutal and unpredicted irruption of 'the war to end all wars'. If only, we are led to think, this accident had not happened; and yet – there are consolations, for without it we would not have had the poetry, which affirms, in the words of one of his poems, an England which 'is all we know and live by, and we trust / She is good and must endure, loving her so'.

But behind this story is another one, less simple, but also less dependent upon 'accident' for its rationale. For that word, we may note, crops up too frequently in Thomas's spiritual autobiography not to be charged with unspoken meanings. And in this version, Thomas's is no mere personal hard-luck story, but a symptomatic destiny. Like his poetry, it inscribes everywhere, not just a private experience, but the crisis of a generation.

The contradictions of his language, of the sensibility his poems delineate, define the dilemma of a middle-class liberal individualism under strain, faced with the prospect of its own redundancy in the changed world of a new era, and struggling, with remarkable intensity and integrity, to understand the flux in which it is to go down. For it is not only the individual here who is in crisis. Rather it is the age itself, of which his personal 'accidents' are an expression, shaping up, in the long perspectives of history, to a larger rationality. That Thomas became one of the most articulate voices of this crisis arises in part, of course, from the 'accident' of his literary talent (though it is surely no accident that many of his literary contemporaries came from the same or similar backgrounds, and followed related paths). It arises too, and most importantly, however, from his 'accidental' situation at a point where a great many of the contradictions of the age happen to intersect. Thomas's death for a handful of English dirt in 1917 is not, in any real sense, an accident, but the logical outcome of the strains in the idea of England itself.

The play between London birth and Welsh allegiance is the key to understanding the idea of England in Thomas's work. For the two extremes open up that expanse of countryside which stretches between them as a third, *ideological* terrain, the perpetually disappearing heart of a 'lost' unity and wholeness which has in fact always been an *imaginary* plenitude, a utopian land of lost content which is precisely nowhere. When Thomas wrote of himself in *The South Country* (p. 30) as one of those 'modern people who belong nowhere', this 'nowhere' takes on a kind of positive force like the 'No Man's Land' of which his character Lob is 'one of the lords'. For it is precisely in being no one, at home nowhere, that the superfluous man lays claim to his inheritance. 'England' as a reality is a perpetually

disappearing place, because it *can* exist only as an
ideological construct. 'England' dwells in the interstices
between places, in those gaps and folds in the landscape
into which Lob perpetually disappears, those places
where a meaning may reside which will make sense of
the whole, 'a place of innumerable holes and corners'
such as he writes of in the essay 'England' in 1914, 'a
system of vast circumferences circling round the minute
neighbouring points of home', which, in a revealing
metaphor, is 'spun out from such a centre into something
large or infinite, solid or aery, according to each man's
nature and capacity' (*LS* pp. 91–111).

For 'England', Thomas suggests in that essay, is not a
fact of nature, a given thing which has abided unchanged
for a thousand years, but the product of a fractured,
divisive and often violent history. The 'foundation of
patriotism' he says 'begins with security', which often
had to be won by the sword: 'Men forgot that the English
race came once upon a time to Britain and made it
England. They were preparing to think of Britain as
rising out of the sea at Heaven's command, with the
sovereignty of the sea.' The Old English poetry, however,
'above all . . . tells me of the making of landmarks and
the beginning of historic places. Of such things has
England gradually been made, not lifted at one stroke
by Heaven's command out of the azure main.'

Writing of the contemporary response to the War, he
records drily how such ideological constructs are manu-
factured, for 'In print men become capable of anything.
The bards and journalists say extraordinary things. I
suppose they do it to encourage the others. They feel
that they are addressing the world; they are intoxicated
with the social sense.' 'England' is not, in fact, a unitary
object, but a collection of subjective experiences, of
individual lives lived in particular places, which can
never be experienced in their totality by anyone. It is

precisely for this reason that the concept of 'England' can be manipulated by the ideology mongers. If we are to understand how and why Thomas's work has been conscripted to an essentially reactionary cult of 'England' and 'Englishness' by the heirs of those 'bards and journalists' he so despised, we need to take into account how other forces were cutting across the ideology of national unity, everywhere raising contradictory currents and eddies.

In the years of Thomas's childhood, the concepts of 'England' and 'Britain' were under strain. The Irish 'Home Rule' movement, as we have seen, elicited a powerful response in the young Thomas, and he recalls in *The Childhood* how, as a child, he delighted in the defiance of Scott's Rhoderick Dhu against the Saxon (pp. 58–9). For 'England', as an ideological concept, depended for its hegemony upon the subjugation of a number of other peoples and nations to produce the effect of an unproblematic 'Englishness'. Thomas's *Literary Pilgrim in England* has sections, without comment, on Scott, Burns and Stevenson, and its very emphasis on the multitude of actual local loyalties to which writers have looked subverts the very idea of 'England' on which it is premised. His anthology *This England* likewise carries the ironic comment that he was 'never aiming at what a committee from Great Britain and Ireland might call complete'. The insistent localism in Thomas's work, given its clearest articulation in the essay 'England', is itself one mode of resistance to the dominant ideology of the age. 'England' was used almost as early for this island as 'Britain', he says there. A poem such as 'The Combe' reveals with a sly hint of discrimination just how much both words are in crisis.

'Britain', after all, has an imperial dimension to it, the term used to amalgamate the peoples of these islands under a more or less accepted sceptre, and to define that Empire which in the jingoist atmosphere that accompanied and followed the Boer War was often referred to as 'Greater Britain'. But there is another, more subversive dimension to the idea of Britain, which takes us back to 'the matter of Britain' in that legendary darkness which preceded the English and ultimately the Roman Empire too – a Britain of obscure and hidden corners before Empire had brought it under the semblance of rule, surviving now only in the swarthy, taciturn peoples of Wales and the West. It is just such a dark backward that the combe seems to represent.

It is, firstly, a landscape peopled actively by no one ('no one scrambles over the sliding chalk'); both closed off, denied utterance, like the poet himself, its 'mouth . . . stopped with bramble, thorn and briar', and excluding, keeping even winter's sun and summer's moon 'quite shut out'. Yet its obscurity could be penetrated, the poet's eye remarks, picking out a possible route down the half precipices of its sides, 'with roots / And rabbit holes for steps'. This doubleness is compounded by its primordial darkness, for 'It was ever dark, ancient and dark'. This darkness is not only excluding but also consolatory, a repository of meanings preserved, out of easy access, for the loving and persistent seeker, just as 'the missel thrush that loves juniper' manages to penetrate its thickets (the bird's name subtly links it with the Celtic druids who also valued mistletoe). This ancient darkness had, thus, a positive value, concentrated in its one true indigenous inhabitant:

> But far more ancient and dark
> The Combe looks since they killed the badger there,
> Dug him out and gave him to the hounds,
> That most ancient Briton of English beasts.

The tension between 'Briton' and 'English' is revealing. What has now been destroyed is an antiquity which is both alien and familiar, remote and intimate. As an 'ancient Briton', the badger represented that which remained most authentic and original at the core of Englishness, something which preceded the *word* 'English'. Its destruction has violated and betrayed that core.

From being a positive, in its ancientness, 'Briton' has now taken on the superficial, jingo quality of a word that proclaims imperial pretensions. Just as Lob's antiquity goes back beyond Norman and Saxon and Roman conquests, so the badger becomes the figure of an aboriginal heart of England endangered by the new, shallow and unfounded discourses of Empire to which the concepts of 'Briton' and 'English' have been recruited. A fictitious character not dissimilar to Thomas, a 'country-bred man with a distinct London accent' who 'wore the everlasting mourning of clerks', in *The Country* in 1913, testifies to this loss, simultaneously reclaiming London for some ancient British significance and dismissing the imperial discourse of 'Greater Britain':

> 'The sublimest thing I know is the sea, and after that London, vast, complex, ancient, restless, and incalculable: I pass through it at night and hear its noises like the wrath and sorrow of lions roaring in bondage, and when I look up the starry sky is like a well in the forest of the city . . . I wonder how many others feel the same, that we have been robbed [. . .] of the small intelligible England of Elizabeth and given the word Imperialism instead. Apollo, Woden, Jehovah, have been put away for the sake of an unsectarian education. No wonder we are languid, fretful, and aimless.' (pp. 1–6)

Thomas is usually perceived either as a nostalgic conservative, or as an aesthete indifferent to politics. His own pronouncements, casually read, often give credence to the idea. In a letter about Wales, for example, written in the same year as *The South Country,* 1908, he observes:

> She is entirely provincial as yet: that is a great part of her charm and opportunity. But she is therefore all the more easily turned into something merely up to date. She must avoid living up to the world's opinion of her as a place where they play football and let lodgings. I do not myself see any chance of a concerted movement, but that is because I am not a social animal.
> (Moore p. 306)

But this disdain for the 'social' carries with it an aroma of regret. Edward Thomas was a child of that professional and administrative middle class whose growth in the last third of the century accompanied the emergence of a paternalist democracy and a bureaucratic imperialism. Such a class found its 'home' in the rapidly expanding suburban villas which stretched out from London and, as E. M. Forster lamented in *Howards End* in 1910, threatened to overwhelm the whole rural hinterland of southern England. Disliking the privileges of the old upper classes, sentimentally loyal to its half-remembered 'roots', this class found an equally sustaining spiritual 'home' in a cautious political liberalism which balanced the ardour of reform with the virtues of stability. Thomas's own father, in his Liberal and Positivist enthusiasms, was a typical figure of this class, a 'social animal' to his fingertips. Almost inevitably, growing up in the relative affluence of an expanding class, Edward Thomas came to despise the simple progressivism of his father's generation, looking, from his privileged, apparently well-cushioned position, for something more emotionally sustaining, less philistine and vulgar than such worldly concerns. In Romantic poetry, and in the nature mysticism of the country writer Richard Jefferies, he

[24]

found one kind of answer. At Oxford he briefly found another, in the aestheticism of Walter Pater.

As Robert Wohl has demonstrated in *The Generation of 1914,* the whole concept of a generational revolt is very much a part of contemporary cultural history, emerging to peculiar intensity in the opening decades of this century. The lament for the lost, sacrificed or betrayed generation quickened, of course, after the Great War, finding expression in such diverse places as Pound's 'Hugh Selwyn Mauberley' and Robert Graves's *Goodbye To All That.* But before the war broke out, Yeats had already written of the nineties writers, in *The Trembling of the Veil,* as 'the Tragic Generation'. Central to all these is the idea of a revolt against the father, and against the collective fathers of bourgeois society. In some cases, the revolt succeeds; in others, the revenge of the fathers is seen as embodied in that war itself, in which so many young men died, in Pound's words 'For an old bitch gone in the teeth, / For a botched civilization'.

In Thomas's case, the revolt against the father took the form familiar in the nineties – a refusal of the whole preoccupation with getting a secure and respectable job and a comfortable suburban home and family, the ambition of his father's generation. Thomas found his father an uncongenial, incomprehensible spirit – someone, he recalls in *The Childhood,* he was astounded as a child to discover had once been a boy like him, who could play marbles like an expert. This grey, sober seriousness he associated with the 'deathly solemnity' of the chapel to which he and his brothers were taken every Sunday, 'cruel ceremonious punishments for the freedom of Monday to Saturday', against which he 'did not rebel, but taking this poison' stiffened into 'a profound quiet detestation of Sunday' and all its works (pp. 31–3).

The holidays the young Thomas spent between the ages of five and fifteen either with his widowed grandmother in Swindon or with family still in South Wales, three or four times a year, roving the countryside, birdnesting, etc., provided him with a sense of an alternative life to that of the suburbs, with all their clerkish grey mediocrity. At the same time, Thomas could see this, as his autobiography reveals, as a journey home, a return to identify with that cultural patrimony among the common people of Wales and the West which his father had abandoned for the shabby gentility of a middle-class existence. Revolt and return to origins thus merge here, in an atavism which is radical in a double sense – a return to roots which is also an uprooting of shallow, surface attachments. Such a return answered that call to the open air Thomas had first excitedly encountered in the writings of the Wiltshireman Richard Jefferies, on whom he modelled his own early nature studies. The young Thomas's dislike of his father's remote, civic pietism here found a literary champion. Rejection of his father's positivism, of his superficial if strongly felt progressivism, his 'social sense' in Thomas's demeaning usage, goes hand in hand with a choosing of an alternative set of father figures.

As *The Childhood* reveals, one such figure was his Uncle Harry, in that 'paradisal' Swindon where the young Thomas spent his holidays, who 'seemed grown up, yet a boy, by the way he laughed, whistled and sang a bit of a gay tune' (p. 46), a womanizer and a rebel. Another such was the old Wiltshire countryman 'Dad' Uzzell, ex-poacher and workman, whom he befriended here as a boy, who became to him a type of the fearless, full-hearted 'yeoman' and labourers he found in Jefferies' writings. But they were matched by other archetypes.

[26]

Philip Henry Thomas's earnest reformism, which evacuated all mystery and ecstasy from life, were things that would hardly appeal to the romantic young man who had discovered Shelley, Wordsworth and Keats as well as Jefferies. Nevertheless, as a boy he imbibed his father's radical Liberalism, so that 'Home Rule took the place of Poetry, and was really an equivalent in so far as it lifted me to vaguely magnificent ideas of good and evil'. Significantly, it was the regicidal, rebellious version of history which appealed to him most, that element which spoke to the child's natural desire to rebel against the omnipotent patriarch: 'the signing of Magna Charta, the Dissolution of the Monasteries, the beheading of Charles I and dethronement of James II, which to me were splendid Liberal events of the past' (p. 105).

At the same time, he found in the charismatic luminaries of the socialist tradition to whom his father introduced him at the Washington Music Hall – Michael Davitt of the revolutionary Irish Land League, 'John Burns, Keir Hardie, and the Socialists' – men who, like Uncle Harry and 'Dad' Uzzell, combined rebellious energy with the authority of the father figure and the imprimatur of the real father as 'glorious, great and good men'. Thomas certainly admired them too, but for qualities quite different from those his father respected. Exuberance, vitality, heroic vigour and a dark passional quality – something that D. H. Lawrence, later Thomas's acquaintance through Eleanor Farjeon, was to turn into a powerful myth of proletarian romance – are what attracted him. Davitt, for example, 'had then just come out of prison, and this probably helped him to a place in my mind with the Pathfinder and Milton's Satan'. John Burns, the militant dockers' leader, 'was another glorious great and good man. I honestly admired his look and voice and was proud to shake hands with him and also to have my middle stump bowled clean out of the ground by him once on Clapham Common' (pp. 105–6).

What appealed to him in such men he found too in such figures as 'Dad' Uzzell, as is revealed in the unpublished essay called 'Dad', quoted by George Thomas in *Edward Thomas: A Portrait*. It was an anarchic, subversive joy in life, a casual illegality and an almost pagan disrespect for privilege and property, a natural egalitarianism and a wisdom that derived from practical experience in the school of necessity:

> But in knowledge of nature beyond that required in poaching – which is very considerable – Dad was even more erudite . . . He certainly had no intention of allowing the old lore concerning herbs to die out . . . Such knowledge as he was full of is fast-decaying . . . he might have made a doctor as well as a poacher . . .
>
> In modern history as it affected his class he was well informed as ever . . . He was bitter against the Church and State though a more truly orthodox man never breathed, and insisted that there was a separate system of law for rich and poor. When bread was a shilling a loaf and men earned less than ten shillings from a long week's work, his father or some other relation was among the most bitterly rebellious against a system that could tolerate such things. Every man poached then, and his family with the rest . . . (pp. 14–16)

Poaching, trespassing, casual contempt for the law, are here the popular virtues, expressing a strenuous and acerbic class-consciousness, to be set against the stuffy respectability of decent, God-fearing Liberals like his father, whose patronizing reformism only muffled the real antagonisms of a class-divided society. Thomas wrote this in 1895. By the end of the first decade of the new century, his own disappointed hopes and growing desperation had combined with a larger social and economic crisis to reawaken such radical sentiments. In 1909, even the placid surface of the English pastoral is ruffled, not for the only time, in *The South Country,* by hints of a darker, more troubled vision of England. Discussing a country house, Thomas points out the price that has to be paid for preserving the idyll of 'England' as an undemandingly unitary realm, happily removed from conflict:

> Only a thousand years of settled continuous govern-ment, of far-reaching laws, of armies and police, of roadmaking, of bloody tyranny and tyranny that poisons quietly without blows, could have wrought earth and sky into such a harmony. It is a thing as remote from me here on the dusty road as is the green evening sky . . . [But] the man in the manor house . . . is a puzzle to me, while the sky is always a mystery with which I am content. At such an hour the house and lawns and trees are more wonderfully fortified by the centuries of time than by the walls and gamekeepers. They weave an atmosphere about it . . . and yet an inevitable conflict ensues in the mind between this respect and the feeling that it is only a respect for surfaces, that a thousand years is a heavy price to pay for the maturing of park and house and gentleman, especially as he is most likely to be a well-meaning parasite on those who are concerned twenty-four hours a day about the difficulty of living and about what to do when they are alive. (*SC*, p. 121)

In 1909, Thomas was himself thus concerned, and shamefully aware too that in earning his living by writing about such scenes he was himself a parasite on a parasite, an apologist for those surfaces and that 'tyranny that poisons quietly without blows'. Thomas may well be, as Andrew Motion suggests, like Lob, as 'English as this gate, these flowers, this mire'. But gates, as that poem subtly suggests, are demarcations of ownership, shutting out the property-less true-born Englishman from the landscape which is his rightful inheritance. One major element in constructing the 'fortified' Englishness of *The South Country* is, after all, the enclosure system which deprived Lob's fore-bears of their common lands, their shared mire. Part of Lob's appeal is that he refuses to accept such enclos-ures, keeping old paths open, insisting to the poet, of one such overgrown pathway. '"Nobody can't stop 'ee. It's / A footpath, right enough."' And Lob's role as a pathfinder suggests a link with that Michael Davitt whose solution to the Irish land problem was a revolu-tionary one – burn out the English landlords.

When Thomas was born in 1878 the Victorian hey-day was over, and a process set under way by the victory at Waterloo had almost reached its climax. The concentration and then the decline of English agricul-ture, which was the ironic result of British maritime hegemony throughout the developing world, was now irreversible. Four-fifths of British wheat was now imported from cheaper colonial granaries. The collapse of agricultural prices in the 1870s had brought to an end the era of country-house building. The rundown of the land, the demoralization of the farmers, and the poverty of the agricultural labourers, now the lowest paid of any large category of workers, created that landscape of picturesque abandon which is recognizably Thomas's own, and that attitude among its inhabitants which Thomas romanticized in a figure like Lob. Thomas's 'Heart of England', in what is significantly one of his own favourite metaphors, had a maggot at the core. As Paul Thompson records in *The Edward-ians: The Remaking of British Society* (1977):

Britain in the 1900s was the most urbanized country in the world. Under a quarter of its people lived in rural districts and a mere seven per cent of its workforce was

engaged in agriculture. The great wave of rural im-
migration into the towns was near its end. Already the
populations of Germany and the United States, now
challenging British industrial supremacy, had well-
surpassed Britain's forty-four millions, but a third of
their workers still remained on the land. Ruthless
urbanization had been one of the foundations of
Britain's greater wealth.

Left to the mercies of the market, unprotected by
state subsidies, the Edwardian countryside was eco-
nomically and socially moribund.

The laconic wisdom of a Lob, and the overgrown
paths of a once populous countryside, thus both alike
register the passage through people and places
of an impersonal economic destiny. As Thompson
caustically observes: 'Most labourers swallowed
their pride and hid their smouldering anger in a
servile but stubborn taciturnity. They worked in
an English countryside which was never more beautiful
or quiet, the great uncut hedges, abundant with
flowers and small animals, arching over empty lanes:
the beauty of decay' (p. 45).

Thomas's writings are full of the imagery of rural
desecration, of houses falling into decay and path-
ways overgrown, communities half effaced or hiding
from intruders. The book of essays *Rose Acre Papers*
assumed an unexpectedly political edge when it was
reprinted in an altered form in 1910 – its privatized,
unworldly 1902 version taking on a discreet but unmistakable resonance as social criticism. 'Caryatids',
for example, offers an overwrought but powerful depic-
tion of field women singing, picking stones, reaping,
'keeping the generations of undespairing sorrow un-
broken' (p. 5) amidst a landscape whose 'wreck of a
sunset . . . scattered round them' (p. 6) gives the lie to
the pastoral version of labour. 'An Autumn House'

[31]

evinces 'Everywhere, the languid perfumes of corruption' (p. 93).

'Isoud with the White Hands' presents an image of pastoral mystery which is charming and attractive in its refusal of the great public highway: 'That road could lead nobody to Rome . . . Then it entered gently into the secret places of the land. On either side the fields and woods lay open . . . beheld in all their divinity' (p. 175). But these roads to 'nowhere' (p. 179) carry their price, as we learn when we hear of the face of the woman glimpsed later in a 'meaningless London crowd' (p. 185). The magical emptiness of the land and the overcrowded meaninglessness of the city are intimately linked. On the one hand, the landscape withdraws into itself, secretively, as, in 'February in England', he 'seemed to be on the eve of a revelation' only to be disappointed when 'In a short time the common look of things returned' (p. 76). Ash trees beside a distant pool seem to conceal some magic: 'Some "potent spirit" was surely hidden among their boughs; as we approached them, indeed, we expected to discover their secret. But on passing underneath all had fled except a whimpering of the breeze' (p. 77). On the other hand, there is what follows this failed revelation, a hellish vision of the city as an abode of inhuman and dehumanized titans.

Everywhere the face of the land is blighted by industrial expansion, the explosion of the slums, and the slow encroachment of the suburbs. Such suburbanization of the countryside provided Thomas with many images of personal dispossession, as he saw the pastoral scenes associated with childhood epiphanies, as he says in *The South Country,* enclosed and built over 'for all the unknown herd, strange to one another, strange to everyone else, that filled the new houses spreading over the land' (p. 84). The sense of a personal fall from grace, of expulsion from the Eden of childhood, was thus intimately interwoven with a social dis-possession.

By the 1900s, depopulation of the land had produced a rural class which was the attenuated residue of the old yeomanry celebrated by Jefferies, and a new urban proletariat still half aware of its agrarian past, but 'living in no ancient way', with 'no tradition about them', such as Thomas described in *The Heart of England.* Among such a displaced mass, the dislocation of the old culture, the restructuring of social life demanded by the town, the decline in real wages and the growth of unemployment during the first decade of the century ushered in an epoch which Thomas described, in a review in the *Daily Chronicle* on 13 January 1908, as 'a centrifugal age, in which principles and aims are numerous, vague, uncertain, confused, and in conflict'. Thomas's 1909 study, *Richard Jefferies,* throws some interesting light on his attitude to these changes.

The Jefferies of this portrait is no simple 'child of the soil' but 'country blood with a difference', for 'both grandfathers had been dipped in London, and had followed there the trade of printing'. His mother, 'in spite of her good butter, was not a countrywoman, and she was soured by the life of one'; and Jefferies himself, like Thomas, was drawn from an early age by the lure of Fleet Street. But Thomas's picture of Jefferies' Wilt-shire is equally informed by a precise historical sense, recording the long slow transformation of social life he witnessed, not just as 'a watcher of birds and animals', or even a 'student of human life' or 'mystic' but, as Thomas stresses, as a 'critic of social conditions'.

The account of Jefferies' career emphasizes its symp-tomatic quality (*RJ* ch. v *passim,* pp. 80-91). The young man who wrote letters to *The Times* in 1872, attacking Joseph Arch's trade union organizing and the 'ingrat-itude' of the agricultural labourer ('lucid, forcible and

[33]

simple exposition', Thomas says, of 'the ideas of the tenant-farming class') was to grow into the author of the last essays on the agricultural problem, 'as bitter against things as they are ordained by the landowners as he used to be against their opponents'. The young Jefferies, inveighing against the corruptions of drink and 'communistic ideas', had already glimpsed the real cause of rural immiseration: the growing impact of foreign imports. Lamenting that '"The country grows more republican year by year . . . the old social links are gone and no new ones have sprung up"', he found, too, '"a marked increase of independence"'. That rural labourers '"have more and more in common with mechanic and navvy"' could also be a cause for hope. As early as 1875, Thomas observes, on a matter that would have had immediate personal relevance, given his own family connections, he found in the men of the Great Western Railway Factory at Swindon an intelligence 'strongly contrasting with the agricultural poor . . . [and] is "tempted to declare" this class of educated mechanics the "protoplasm or living matter out of which modern society is evolved"'.

Throughout his account, Thomas is keen to discern the contradictory moments in which an ideology unwittingly gives itself away. Thus of the early essays collected in *Hodge and his Masters*, Thomas remarks: 'As yet he was hardly free from the ideas of his class, and he did what was expected of him.' Yet even here a book 'on the whole partisan' nevertheless 'tells in the end by its weight of wide and intimate knowledge', pulling in directions quite at odds with its polemic intent, and Thomas is at pains to indicate this tension. Its 'Conclusion' 'has a plain statement of the man-made unhappiness of the aged labourer' which 'attempts no solution; it lays no blame; yet it does throw the door

[34]

open to a draught most uncomfortable to receive at the end of a book that would have been, without it, one to keep in good spirits the investors in things as they are'. Jefferies 'does not dwell on the possibility that there is something deeply wrong, if not in the region of party politics, when the land is left idle and only the men who could till it suffer'.

Only in the 1880s was Jefferies drawn to that 'venturing into politics' which would have appalled his younger self. 'The labour question, he sees, is every-where . . . Money is more and more' (*RJ*, p. 292ff). When, in 'After the County Franchise', he proposed compul-sory purchase of the land by the community, a system of national insurance, and an extension of rural demo-cracy through 'a village council that shall represent the people, in place of a Board of Guardians which is "land and money simply"', he was following through what Thomas calls 'a naïve and most troublesome logic': 'He even asks, Can an owner of this kind of property be permitted to refuse to sell? Which is a pertinent but saucy question for a yeoman's son to ask.' When the garrulous Wheat in 'Saint Guido' rebukes men '"because you do not share us among you without price or difference; because you do not share the great earth among you fairly"', Thomas observes wryly: 'It is naughty, socialistic Wheat.' The social criticism and the nature mysticism, he sees, are all of a piece, as he stresses in discussing 'The Wiltshire Labourer', which sees rural vagrancy as a direct product of insecurity of tenure:

> They 'deserve' settled homes. 'Deserve'! The word is revolutionary, and that Jefferies should soberly point out what a class of men deserves, as if that were some reason for giving it, marks an interesting change from the year of his letters to *The Times;* it marks the intrusion of his ideals into practical matters.

[35]

Appearing in the same year as Beveridge's report on unemployment and an act of Parliament establishing national labour exchanges, and amidst the widespread canvassing of land nationalization as a rational solution to agricultural decline, Thomas's own book marks an intrusion into practical matters. *The South Country,* published in the same year as *Richard Jefferies,* for all its rustic charm, devotes a whole chapter to the evils of unemployment and alienation in the work process. Thomas's own development follows Jefferies' trajectory. 'Nature' means 'the land' and 'land' means money – poverty and wealth, work and unemployment. 'A mile of it is worth a guinea', says the young girl in 'Up in the Wind'. 'Man and Dog' likewise show Thomas's grasp of the transformations of rural England to be unsentimental and precise. A panorama of social history since the 1870s is concentrated into one sentence of retrospect attributed to the old vagrant day-labourer he meets in the woods, now reduced to flint-picking and pulling up dockweed:

> His mind was running on the work he had done
> Since he left Christchurch in the New Forest, one
> Spring in the 'seventies, – navvying on dock and line
> From Southampton to Newcastle-on-Tyne, –
> In 'seventy-four a year of soldiering
> With the Berkshires, – hoeing and harvesting
> In half the shires where corn and couch will grow.

Of Novalis, Thomas wrote in *Maurice Maeterlinck* in 1911: 'Having said that "Philosophy is, properly speaking, homesickness, the desire to be at home in the world," he says no more' (p. 122). But Thomas does say more. In a seminal essay D. W. Harding detected in Thomas's poetry a condition he diagnosed as 'nostalgia': 'the feeling of distress for no localized, isolated cause, together with the feeling that one's environment is strange, and vaguely wrong and unacceptable'. Dispossession, displacement, vagrancy in Thomas's poems may take on the appearance of a metaphysical condition, but they have their roots in a precise historical experience – not in any localized, isolated cause, but in a whole interlocking network of social transformations. Thomas's generation of intellectuals had grown up in the expectation of plenty. Entering the labour market at the turn of the century, they found that the world did not, in fact, lie all before them, that the literary or academic career was not as easily sustained in the changed conditions of the 1900s as it had been in their fantasies. Unfitted to the world of strenuous, unrewarding activities in which they had to earn a living, such men turned back upon themselves with a heightened sense of their own marginality and irrelevance. Whereas women such as Helen Thomas could find in the Suffrage movement a sense of political identity which connected with and made intelligible their personal lives, men such as Edward Thomas, reared on the 1890s rejection of politics, found it difficult to respond to the utilitarian values of middle-class reform. To many such, possessed by a feeling of general fraudulence with no clear external cause or remedy, the deepening social crisis of the first decade of the century offered, in the awakening of working-class militancy, an objective correlative of their own discontent which engaged, too, with the values of the kind of revolutionary and aesthetically oriented socialism of William Morris on which they had been reared. Many espoused radical causes: socialism, feminism, Home Rule. For Thomas, too, the period of the last Liberal government and of the social upheaval its palliative reforms failed to avert gave a new and personal intensity to ideas with which he had been familiar since childhood.

In 1909 the House of Lords had vetoed the Liberal budget by an overwhelming majority, in protest against a modest proposal for taxing landowners. This clearly unconstitutional act of blatant class self-interest gave the Chancellor Lloyd George and the radicals in the Government the chance to act. In July of that year he had delivered the speech at Limehouse, to an audience of appreciative East Enders, that many in the ruling classes had seen as a direct incitement to riot, attacking dukes and landowners as parasites whose unearned income came from blackmail, 'a piece of insolence which no intelligent man would tolerate'. In Newcastle four months later he carried the demagogy further, speaking of the House of Lords' veto on his budgetary proposals:

> Let them realize what they are doing. They are forcing a Revolution, and they will get it. The Lords may decree a revolution, but the people will direct it. If they begin, issues will be raised that they little dream of . . . Who made ten thousand people owners of the soil, and the rest of us trespassers in the land of our birth? . . . Where did the table of that law come from? Whose finger inscribed it? *(Better Times,* 1910, pp. 151, 174–5)

On 6 January 1912 *The Times* warned that 'the public must be prepared for a conflict between Labour and Capital, or between employers and employed, upon a scale as has never occurred before.' Its editorials throughout the period make it clear that *The Times* knew which side it was on. In July of that year the ruling class's respect for constitutionality and the rule of law was revealed as the sham it always had been by the speech of the Conservative leader himself, Bonar Law, at Blenheim Palace to a large and enthusiastic meeting of the faithful. The Liberal government, he said, was 'a revolutionary committee which seized by fraud upon despotic power', and their opposition to it could no longer be confined within constitutional channels, for 'there are things stronger than Parliamentary majorities'. If Home Rule was to be imposed on Ulstermen, he continued, 'they would be justified in resisting by all means in their power, including force . . . I can imagine no length of resistance to which Ulster will go in which I shall not be ready to support them'. (*The Times*, 29 July 1912). In such an atmosphere, even a poet with no 'social sense' like Thomas could still have the intolerance of the intelligent man to such a 'piece of insolence'.

There is an increasingly edgy tone to Thomas's reviewing from about 1908 onwards – a social unease with radical leanings – which reaches its peak about the time of his breakdown in September 1911. In February of that year he wrote in *The Bookman* of 'the inevitable exile' and the 'feeling something like paralysis' of the poet in modern society, and hailed William Morris's 'faithful Socialist' attempt to read the ambiguous message of the March Wind, blowing from 'the "shabby hell" of the city', but presaging 'a union between love of one woman and of the world'. In January he had selected as 'one of the essential things' in Stephen Cunningham Graham's book *A Vagabond in the Caucasus* a remark which obviously cut deep into his own sense of social vagrancy:

> You English have forgotten that you are brothers. Money has come between you, and money has made you work. You are all gathered together not out of love, but out of hate. In England, gregariousness; in Russia, conviviality. (*DC* 9 January 1911)

A passage written about the same time in *Lafcadio Hearn,* published in 1912, speaks contemptuously of 'European civilization, with "unlimited individuality" to starve or purchase a peerage', and adds:

Hearn saw the horrors of this free society, but dreaded Socialism, which he called a "reversion towards the primitive conditions of human society." . . . He foresaw "a democracy more brutal than any spartan oligarchy" . . . and this he confused with Socialism. (p. 86)

The peerage was, of course, a crucial political issue in the two general elections of 1910, called because the House of Lords had obstructed the passage of radical legislation and in particular what came to be known as Lloyd George's 'People's Budget'. Talk of starvation and socialism was not just rhetoric in 1910–12. The accelerating inflation which characterized the whole pre-war period produced a doubling in the rate of increase of the cost of living from 4 to 5 per cent per annum in 1908 to 9 per cent between 1909 and 1913, provoking widespread labour unrest. The number of days per annum lost in strikes multiplied from something, on average, above two million in 1908, something just below this in 1910–11, to a momentous forty-one million in 1912.[1] In 1911 there were widespread stoppages among dockers, seamen, transport and railway workers, some of which culminated in rioting and even, on occasions, in bloodshed. A ten-month-long miners' strike in Thomas's own South Wales, accompanied by riots, begun late in 1910, was met by the movement of London police and then troops into the area.[2] Thomas's essay 'Mothers and Sons' in *Rest and Unrest* (1910) is an oblique homage to

---

[1] Committee on Industry and Trade, *Survey of Industrial Relations* (HMSO, 1926); *Ministry of Labour Gazette; Fifteenth Abstract of Labour Statistics of the UK* (Cmnd 6228, 1912).
[2] Henry Pelling, *A History of British Trades Unionism* (1963), pp. 123–48. Herbert Tracy (ed.), *The Book of the Labour Party* (1925), vol. 1, pp. 191–201. Sidney and Beatrice Webb (eds.), *History of British Trade Unionism* (1920), p. 690. Lord Askwith, *Industrial Problems and Disputes* (1920), p. 155.

the communities in which such a struggle arose. The crisis deepened in 1912, so that many people shared the conclusion of the king himself, opening the Buckingham Palace Conference on Ulster, when he spoke of 'The trend . . . surely and steadily towards an appeal to force' so that 'today the cry of civil war is on the lips of the most responsible and sober of my people'.[3] Civil war was not a prospect, at this moment, confined to the special province of Ireland; rather the extremity of the Irish situation seemed to reflect a tendency to disintegration incipient to the whole 'United' Kingdom.

Thomas was not immune to these events – not only because his populist sentiments led him into inevitable sympathy with the cause of labour, but because he too was a victim of the inflationary movement that was undermining the real value of wages. Inflation during these three years had already subverted a tenuous financial equilibrium to the point at which, between 1910 and 1912, Thomas was forced into the superhuman effort that produced twelve books and, in September 1911, the nervous breakdown which was the inevitable culmination of overwork and chronic anxiety. The crisis was compounded by the birth of his third child and the financial and emotional burden of the new house at Wick Green in Hampshire into which they had moved in 1909 (they left in 1913). This is the house of the poem 'Wind and Mist' which Thomas came to hate as the scene of his greatest misfortunes. The poem, written in April 1915, recalls the period of his nervous breakdown; the anguish of that period has been sublimed into a sense of metaphysical persecution: the lonely self,

[3] Tracy, op. cit., p. 196. On the general background to the period's radicalism, George Dangerfield's classic narrative, *The Strange Death of Liberal England*, remains unexcelled.

carrying the burden of his 'furniture and family', looks out of the windows at a world repossessed by the mist which has cut him off from all contact and solace. The soil is recalcitrant, unyielding; life itself, barren, even though a child is born there; and the house is beset by a wind which threatens the last tenuous security of a life 'lived in clouds, on a cliff's edge almost':

> But flint and clay and childbirth were too real
> For this cloud castle. I had forgot the wind.
> Pray do not let me get on to the wind.
> You would not understand about the wind.
> It is my subject, and compared with me
> Those who have always lived on the firm ground
> Are quite unreal in this matter of the wind.
> There were whole days and nights when the wind and I
> Between us shared the world, and the wind ruled
> And I obeyed it and forgot the mist.
> My past and the past of the world were in the wind.

It is not necessary to foist a crude allegorical meaning on the symbolism of wind and mist. They stand for vast, impersonal forces beyond individual control, in a world where 'The flint was the one crop that never failed'. It would be equally foolish, though, to ignore the extent to which the symbolism is imbued with personal, obsessive intensity by the experience of economic insecurity and the exhausting struggle to survive in an unaccommodating world. Significantly, the poem ends with a reference to 'the house-agent's young man' who is trying to sell the house for the poet.

Since graduating from Oxford in 1900 Thomas had worked non-stop, sometimes reviewing as many as thirty books a week, for a variety of newspapers and journals. The work was unremitting, but had to be supplemented by producing the books that took up most of his time during these years. Some of them have a peculiar deadening flatness that could only compound his depression, emphasizing the squandering of a talent of which much had been expected. The sharpening economic crisis meant that the financial returns on this work may actually have declined, in real terms, during the second half of the decade. The period is summed up in the title of one of the best of these books, *Rest and Unrest* (1910), a collection of essays which shows Thomas finding an affinity between his own desperation and the stirrings of a wider world against its exploitation, and fluctuating between resentful revolt and quietistic resignation. It may be that personal pathology led to that breakdown in 1911; but it is scarcely possible to extract the personal crisis from the social matrix that cast this individual up to this particular destiny. In a sense, the private catastrophe was itself the function of a more widespread malaise.

It is not surprising, then, that by 1911 Thomas was on the edge of breakdown from overwork and the perpetual strain and frustration of unfulfilled ambitions. A suicide attempt in that year, fictionalized in 'The Attempt' in *Light and Twilight,* was succeeded by actual collapse in September. Living on his nerves, writing endlessly, sometimes several thousand words a day, he had reached the state of anomie recorded in the poem 'The Long Small Room', a sense of the pointlessness and fatuity of his own life, constructed as arbitrarily and accidentally (he was, after all, an 'accidental' Cockney) as the room in which and of which he writes: 'No one guessed / What need or accident made them so build.' But, unlike that room, this 'accidental' life is disliked, resented, coming by the end of the poem to seem nothing more than an instrument for almost automatic writing, in the powerful metonymy which reduces the self to a mere hand, crawling crablike across the page, resting briefly each night on the

[43]

pillow, then crawling on again towards age. The sudden displacement with which the poem ends, in shifting to an isolated image of time running out beyond the personal life, marginalizes, chastens that life, as earlier, it had been marginalized by moon, mouse and sparrow that saw and heard what went on in the house but '[kept] / The tale for the old ivy and older brick'. Supersession is not something yet to come; it is already here, in the sense that human lives are just passing through, without ever understanding, the house in which they briefly live. In Thomas's poetry, the old house, as we shall see, is a powerful image for this sense of social dispossession. Although they inhabit the house of their culture, superfluous men such as he do not own it or share in its significances. Those meanings have passed elsewhere, are not now available to the one who wants to decipher them. The self is reduced to a mere perpetuator, a moving hand, that carries on a tradition in which it does not really participate. He may have liked the idiosyncratic room. Nevertheless, it has become a 'dark house', a place of bondage and untransmitted messages, lost tales belonging to a departed 'they'. And in fact the poet too has already quite literally moved on, looks back from another house in painful recognition of his incomprehension and powerlessness:

> When I look back I am like moon, sparrow and mouse
> That witnessed what they could never understand
> Or alter or prevent in the dark house.
> One thing remains the same – this my right hand
>
> Crawling crab-like over the clean white page,
> Resting awhile each morning on the pillow,
> Then once more starting to crawl on towards age.
> The hundred last leaves stream upon the willow.

The discrepancy between witnessing and understanding here is a crucial one, for it issues directly into that other contrast, between all the endless, futile busyness and the actual inability to alter or prevent anything. The fatalism of this poem, of this life, focused in the grotesque image of a crab-like hand detached from any human wholeness, arises precisely from the looking subject's inability to make sense of something he looks at, in self-division, as the meaningless activity of an alien object. Yet at the same time, as Thomas found the young Jefferies seeing more than he realized in his early essays, the poem obscurely grasps that it is in that inability, that refusal perhaps, to understand, that the problem has its source.

That understanding could be found only by a 'venturing into politics' similar to Jefferies' own. It is something, in fact, which Thomas's prose, even at its most escapist, finds itself continually tentatively approaching, and then shying away from. His most explicit renunciation of politics, for example, occurs in a playfully ironic passage in *The South Country* which dismisses much more that bourgeois 'civilization' holds dear. There is more than a tinge of 1890s *Weltschmerz,* undercut by self-deprecation, in the fastidious aesthetic distaste with which he dismisses a banal world. But there is at the same time a hint that, in this conscious refusal of 'knowledge' and 'wisdom', lies the source of that estrangement from an uncapturable 'real' self which is here not so much the bane as the delight of the pursuer:

> And so I travel, armed only with myself, an avaricious and often libertine and fickle eye and ear, in pursuit, not of knowledge, not of wisdom, but of one whom to pursue is never to capture. Politics, the drama, science, racing, reforms and preservations, divorces, book clubs, – nearly everything which the average (oh! so mysterious average man, always to b met but never

met) and the superior and the intelligent man is always thinking of, I cannot grasp; my mind refuses to deal with them; and when they are discussed I am given to making answers like 'In Kilve there is no weathercock.' I expect there are others as unfortunate, superfluous men such as the sanitation, improved housing, police, charities, medicine of our wonderful civilization save from the fate of the cuckoo's foster brothers. They will perhaps follow my meanders and understand. (p. 6)

The *faux-naïveté* of this contempt for 'politics' is itself inscribed with all the indirection of which it speaks. It is a common enough inflection of radical attitudes in what, in an early review, Thomas called 'this decadent age of political and artistic contortionists' *(Daily Chronicle,* 12 September 1903). To remain free from such contortions, the artist assumes a pose of abstention which itself becomes a form of political statement. This is, characteristically, the attitude summed up by the concept Thomas has here borrowed from Turgenev, whom he admired – the 'superfluous man'.

The superfluous man is a common figure in Thomas's prose, and always comes armed with this political obliquity. He speaks for himself in chapter vi of *The South Country* and in *The Country,* and he has a chapter named after him in *The Happy-Go-Lucky Morgans.* (He is, in fact, that Aurelius whose remarks about the manufacture of London fog are quoted above, which suggests that he can, when he wants to, see through the fog of evasion with which his identity and his place in society are invested.) Noticeably, in that passage from *The South Country* above, Thomas's metaphor subverts our expectations: the superfluous man is not the cuckoo in the nest but the dispossessed rightful inheritor, equivocally retained by a civilization guiltily unable to abolish him totally.

[46]

Such indirection is characteristic of the superfluous man, not just as the content of what he says, but in his very existence as a narrative figure. He usually occurs in the prose as a semi-fictional projection of the author's own point of view, as is the case of the clerk in *The Country* or the sceptical patriot of the essay 'England'. He is allowed to speak for himself, yet he seems little more than a mouthpiece. But, though a mouthpiece, his sentiments are not fully endorsed by the author, who puts a sceptical narrative distance between him and them. Framing them by putting the words into the mouth of an invented character, as with Yeats's Michael Robartes and Owen Aherne, Thomas as the narrator endows both their significance and their origin with a mystery which cannot easily be laid to rest. Yet there is a subliminal bond of affiliation which cannot be denied. We know that, really, he *is* their author, and they carry his authority. The man himself is full of contradictions (some of which are pointed out by the narrator) and provides counter-arguments which refute (or appear to) his own previous statements.

This 'ghostly double', as he is called in *The Icknield Way,* is not simply an antithetical representation of the self like Yeats's *Hic* and *Ille,* for there is no consistent set of oppositions. The ambiguity is, in fact, the essence of his condition. It is precisely in the contradictoriness, the evasions of responsibility, the refusal to be pinned down, that his meaning lies. The superfluous man in *The South Country* is not so much the pursued other as the self with whom one comes 'armed', a confusion which is compounded by the suggestion that it is the 'average man' who is really elusive. In the poem 'The Other' a similar complication obtains. The pursued self is a rarer and more authentic being than the pursuing narrator, one's 'real' and therefore always elusive identity, and it is the casual and then increasingly desperate pursuer who can be identified with the flippant and indecisive superfluous man. What the poet is really pursuing in 'The Other', in fact, is precisely that 'social' self, able to feel at home in the world, from which all the instincts of egregiousness exclude him. Such a oneness with the world is vouchsafed during this pursuit only amidst the solitude of a sunset which allows him to feel, briefly, 'An old inhabitant of earth'. Thomas himself fluctuates in diagnosing the cause of his estrangement. The vacillation is itself part of the condition.

Writing of the fin-de-siècle decadent, Ernest Dowson, in 1905, for example, Thomas seems to propose the superfluous man as an archetype of a metaphysical alienation, though the terms in which he couches this are redolent with the languorous nihilism of the 1890s:

> Yet is it not clear that Dowson was simply the embodied groan of one brief stage of humanity's long probation on the wheel of Time? . . . To us he seems to have rediscovered regret and all the emotions which the inaccessible and irrecoverable arouse, since he expressed them with a beauty and simplicity which no contemporary equalled . . . Deep within the dark background of them all is the comic, terrible cry of the superfluous man . . . of all their self-pity, self-love, self-hate, of that regret and hunger, for they know not what, which are their only emotions that touched the sublime. (*DC*, 26 May 1905).

This characteristically hovers between being a metaphysical or a historical condition. Yet even at its most metaphysical there is also usually a hint of a social aetiology. In the chapter 'Aurelius, The Superfluous Man' in *The Happy-Go-Lucky Morgans,* for example, 'the superfluous are those who cannot find

[48]

any society with which they are in some sort of harmony', but are enclosed by the circle of their own isolate self-consciousness, 'the magic circle drawn around us all at birth', which will never overlap the circles of other minds among 'the whirling multitudes'. Yet at the same time, they occupy a clear social stratum, as a destiny, if not as a point of origin: 'In a civilization like ours', he says, 'the superfluous abound and even flourish'. Though they may be born in a palace, a cottage or under a hedge, they end up at the tense interface of the two major classes, for, he notes, ironically, 'they neither produce like the poor nor consume like the rich' (pp. 48–50).

In *The Country* he is that clerk who expatiates at length on the cultural and political causes for the modern restlessness and languor. But it is in chapter vi of *The South Country*, 'A Return to Nature' (pp. 77–97), that he presents the most explicitly social account of his condition. Like Thomas, he has Welsh ancestry which looks back to Caermarthenshire; like Thomas's, his father was a clerk who 'thought to better himself, worked hard in the evenings and came to London . . . for a better-paid post'; like Thomas's his childhood was spent 'in Wandsworth in a small street newly built'; like Thomas, he 'went to a middle-class school close by', and felt regret at the strange people in strange new houses, 'spreading over the land'. Like Thomas, he returns to the land to seek a content denied in those suburbs, only to experience a profounder alienation there, repeating his childhood experience of a 'terror that enrolled [him] as one of the helpless, superfluous ones of the earth'. But his diagnosis of this as a social condition is clear:

> 'I realize that I belong to the suburbs still. I belong to no class or race, and have no traditions. We of the suburbs are a muddy, confused, hesitating mass, of

[49]

small courage though much endurance. As for myself, I am world-conscious, and hence suffer unutterable loneliness.'

The confusion, the restlessness, the diffidence, the hesitant circumspection, all alike arise from this contradiction between the world-historical aspirations and the limited class identity. And this identity is specifically one of deracination, disaffiliation. Like Matthew Arnold's 'saving remnant', the internal émigré suffers for the largeness of his soul; but at the same time he is afflicted by a self-contempt which undermines any simple self-romanticizing. He has read too many Russian novels not to feel the pangs of the 'underground man', the remorse and self-laceration which alert him to the fact that his cry is 'comic' as well as 'terrible'. But if he suffers from his intermediate location in a social *space,* the deepest alienation derives from his deadlock in *time.* He suffers from a historical paralysis which denies him a future as well as a past:

'But yet I cannot look forward – there is nothing ahead – just as I cannot look back. My people have not built; they were not settled on the earth; they did nothing; they were oil or grit in a great machine; they took their food and shelter modestly and not ungratefully from powers above that were neither kind nor cruel.'

Not surprisingly, when the narrator sees him again a few years later, he has identified with a class that may have a future, in a march of the unemployed through the London streets. Parched with summer heat, the city offers not a return to nature but to society, for even here nature takes on an alienated cast, debased and degraded at the heart of civil society, the plane trees sharing the suburban blight, looking back to a lost past, 'like so many captives along the streets, shackled to the flagstones, pelted with dust, humiliated, all their rusticity ravished though not forgotten', but also fantasizing a future, like 'the grass [which] was a prophet muttering wild ambiguous things', but only in a voice that 'was very small and came from underground'.

This is a crucial chapter for understanding Thomas's complex attitude to the dilemma of his generation, and its political options. It has all his characteristic ambivalence. On the one hand, speaking in his own voice, he emphasizes the powerlessness and futility of any attempt to change things. Civil society is seen as a vast machine to imprison desire, and even the watcher, the superfluous intellectual who knows this, is only a little freer for his knowledge:

> Some vast machinery plunged and thundered behind the walls, but though they trembled and grew hot, it burst not through. Even so the multitude in the streets . . . roared and moved swiftly and continuously, encaged within walls that are invisible; and they also never burst through. Both are free to do what they are told. All of the crowd seem a little more securely imprisoned than him who watches, because he is aware of his bars; but they move on, or seem to do, on and on, round and round, as thoughtless as the belt of an engine.

Yet on the other hand, as that repeated 'seems' gives away, these 'invisible' walls are human constructions, mind-forged (Blake is an obvious influence behind the vision), and the passage cannot resist muttering its own wild, ambiguous prophecies. The image of a silence surrounding speech, abundant in Thomas's work, here takes on a subtly political cast as an image of the estrangement between individual and mass. By linking with that image of London as a restless sea which we have already encountered in *The Country* it suggests a way out of the impasse. For if 'The roar in which all played a part developed into a kind of silence which not any of these millions could break; the sea does not absorb the little rivers more completely than this silence the voices of men and women, than this solitude their personalities', the metaphor also allows for the idea of an impersonal power that transcends the sum of its parts, and could issue in a revolutionary release of these deadlocked energies:

> There is a more than human force in the movement of the multitude, more than the sum of all the forces in the arched necks, the grinding chest muscles . . . It is hard to understand why they do not sometimes stop one another, to demand where the soul and the soul's business is hid, to snatch away the masks. It was intolerable that they were not known to me, that I was not known to them, that we should go on like waves of the sea, obeying whatever moon it is that sends us thundering on the unscalable shores of night and day. Such force, such determination as moved us along the burning streets might scale Olympus. Where was he who could lead the storming-party?

What is intolerable here is exactly that mutual estrangement which, at the beginning of the book, the narrator had delighted in as the boon of the super-fluous man 'in pursuit of one whom to pursue is never to capture'. The question here gets an answer as evasive as 'In Kilve there is no weathercock', for the narrative throws up, in response, a march of the unemployed, led by 'a tall son of man', which simultaneously responds to the apocalyptic, prophetic tones of the question and reduces them almost to bathos. And yet – not quite. For Thomas preserves his sceptical distance. He may feel that the jeering clerks are accurate in their assess-ments. But he regrets it. His heart is all with the force of the protest and revolt, and that final juxtaposition of comments (which closes the chapter) skilfully and obliquely clinches the effect, reminding us of that other 'son of man' who was also mocked but whose physical exposure and weakness was the source of his revolutionary moral power:

> Comfortable clerks and others of the servile realized that here were the unemployed about whom the newspapers had said this and that – ('a pressing question' – a very complicated question not to be decided in a hurry' – 'it is receiving the attention of some of the best intellects of the time' – 'our special reporter is making a full investigation' – 'who are the genuine and who are the imposters?' – 'connected with Socialist intrigues') – and they repeated the word 'Socialism' and smiled at the bare legs of the son of man and the yellow boots of the orator. Next day they would smile again with pride that they had seen the procession which ended in feeble and violent speeches against the Army and the Rich, in four arrests and an imprisonment. For they spoke in voices gentle with hunger. They were angry and uttered curses. One waved an arm against a palace, an arm that could scarcely hold a revolver even were all the kings sitting in a row to tempt him. In the crowd and disturbance the leader fell and fainted. They propped him in their arms and cleared a space about him. 'Death of Nelson', suggested an onlooker, laughing, as he observed the attitude and the knee-breeches. 'If he had only a crown of thorns . . .' said another, pleased by the group. 'Wants a bit of skilly and real hard work,' said a third.

This passage, in miniature, encapsulates the political ambivalence of Thomas's life and work. Its presence in a book of supposedly bucolic intent is deeply subversive, particularly in a chapter aggressively entitled 'A Return to Nature'. Yet the irony and rueful resignation counterbalance the revolutionary sentiments. The shifting tonalities of the text cancel each other out, in a way which enacts the very paralysis of which Thomas speaks. It is out of this deadlock that the obliquities and indirections of Thomas's poetry issue. This very ambivalence speaks right from, and to, the heart of England, in all its prevarications and evasions, its perpetual deferral of crisis, its delaying of that climacteric moment in which all the debts are called in and the reckoning has to be paid. This is what enables him to appeal both to the Ramblers' Association and the revolutionary poets W. H. Auden and C. Day Lewis, who in 1927 included him in the 'extremely short' catalogue of 'contemporary poets whom we had little or no hope of ever equalling'. When F. R. Leavis in *New Bearings in English Poetry* in the 1930s spoke of Thomas's 'distinctively modern sensibility', it was precisely this complex and discriminating balance of contrary impulses, this sense of a perpetually deferred climax and crisis, which defined the modern. His ambivalence links him, too, to the ambiguities of the Modernist movement itself, for all Andrew Motion's demurrals, to Yeats and Pound (both of whom he reviewed admiringly) and to Eliot, with their strange amalgam of revolt and reaction. For of course the final way in which the political and social crisis of Thomas's England, that great upheaval which not only Thomas but *The Times* itself expected, was deferred was by the outbreak of war in August 1914, as Pound proclaimed with savage indignation in 'Hugh Selwyn Mauberley'. All that slowly accumulating force and determination, capable of storming Olympus, was changed at once into an outburst of patriotism, and spent its revolutionary potential in the mud of Flanders.

When Eleanor Farjeon asked Thomas in 1915 whether he knew what he was fighting for he replied not with the rhetoric of the bard or journalist but with a gesture, indicating that words could not be trusted to be innocent of the 'social sense', picking up a pinch of earth and saying, 'Literally, for this' (*LFY* p. 154).

When Thomas travelled the length and breadth of the
country in 1914 to write those articles about the response to the War, 'England', 'It's a Long, Long Way'
and 'Tipperary', the strongest impression he formed
was of the quiet dignity of the working men queueing
to enlist. '[T]he great majority' of the recruits, he wrote
in 'Tipperary', 'wore dark clothes and caps, had pale
faces tending to leanness, and stood somewhere about
five foot seven. It was only the beginning, some
thought, of a wide awakening to a sense of the danger
and the responsibility. Clean and dirty – some of them,
that is, straight from the factory – of all ages and
features, they were pouring in. Some might be loafers,
far more were workers . . . Here and there a tanned
farm labourer with lighter-coloured, often brownish
clothes, chequered the pale-faced dark company.'

The class emphasis is insistent, and it links the
Thomas prepared to die for a handful of dust with the
Thomas who in 1911 looked to William Morris's
'Message of the March Wind' for its vision of a socialist
insurrection. 'Beside my hate for one fat patriot', he
wrote in one much misunderstood poem, 'My hatred of
the Kaiser is love true'. Politicians and philosophers
cannot judge the matter; newspapers cannot make him
'grow hot / With love of Englishmen'; historians may
rake some deeper meaning out of the ashes 'when
perchance / The phoenix broods serene above their
ken'. But, as in 'Tipperary', the definition of England
lies with those ordinary working men from town and
country who flocked silently to enlist, with what this
poem calls 'the best and meanest Englishmen'. That
this line identifies the 'meanest' *as* the best is confirmed by the section of his anthology *This England*
called 'The Vital Commoners'. There Thomas quotes
with enthusiasm the sermon preached against
'enclosers' by Bishop Hugh Latimer before Edward VI,

with its boast 'My father was a yeoman, and had no lands of his own', its protest that the realm is destroyed by impoverishing such men, and its impassioned plea that the one man who has reduced rents in the whole realm 'not be a phoenix, let him not be alone'. The phoenix rebirth of England Thomas envisages is not achieved by fat patriots, but in the name and interest of what Latimer, in this extract, calls 'the commonwealth'. Even in the essay 'England', Thomas still looks to the revolutionary regicide Milton, to the young Wordsworth excited by the French Revolution, and to the radicals Blake and Hazlitt, for his image of what 'This England' is.

In 1905, writing to Gordon Bottomley of his own self-consciousness, and the 'misery, dissatisfaction, imperfection, perhaps "tragedy" or tragic farce rather' it occasioned, he added that 'only a revolution or a catastrophe or an improbable development can ever make calm or happiness possible for me' (*LGB,* pp. 90–1). Significantly, when John Moore repeats this he omits the word 'revolution', for this is not a Thomas that conforms to Moore's image of an English conservative, patriot and nature lover:

> How thoroughly, how much too thoroughly, he understood himself! It is almost startling to find him thus prophesying his own fate. *'Only a catastrophe or an improbable development can ever make calm or happiness possible for me.'*
>
> So he wrote in 1905. Twelve years later the roaring of the guns before Arras, the uncertainty of living and the carelessness of dying, in some queer way brought to his troubled spirit a kind of calm which was like the stillness of evening; and in that calm he wrote at last what had always been in his heart to write, and doing so was happy and at peace in the midst of war. (Moore, p. 122)

Moore is of course right to suppress the word, for it

clearly has no part in the English tradition, with all its calm continuities and settled assurance. There is no ambiguity in the two poems Thomas included, under an assumed name, in his anthology *This England*, 'The Manor Farm' and 'Haymaking'. The 'Sunday silentness' of the former is untainted by Thomas's loathing of Sunday, of which he spoke in *The Childhood*, its 'season of bliss unchangeable / Awakened from farm and church where it had lain / Safe under tile and thatch for ages since / This England, Old already, was called Merry', unaffected by any sense of a wider awakening. The vision of labour suspended in the latter, the men leaning silent and still on their rakes, about to begin, linking back to Clare and Cobbett, Morland and Crome, is unaffected by memories of Clare's miserable poverty and Cobbett's *Rural Rides*, and the ancientness of the scene is no reproach to the transitory watchers who are framed in the closing lines as if in a picture, but framed, too, by the reality of a labour which alone utters and alone outlives all this pastoral rumination:

> The men, the beasts, the trees, the implements
> Uttered even what they will in times far hence –
> All of us gone out of the reach of change –
> Immortal in the picture of an old grange.

Thomas never resolved, never perhaps even saw, some of the contradictions of his own dilemma; but the clues are everywhere. He was never, as he observed in discussing Shelley, obsessed by 'a passion for reforming the world', but he was 'puzzled to some purpose by the riddles of his own day' (*DC*, 7 October 1902). His death at Arras in 1917 in a way consummated but did not resolve the contradictions which had pervaded his life. In the poetry they exist as lived tensions and anxieties, doubts, hesitations and bewilderment. As such, the poetry embodies a 'subtler moral', in the words of that same review, than any poetry 'in a very obvious way influenced by the spirit of the age'. For the poems, in the words of 'I never saw that land before', 'sing' what his soul 'would not even whisper', using

> as the trees and birds did
> A language not to be betrayed;
> And what was hid should still be hid
> Excepting from those like me made
> Who answer when such whispers bid.

But what whispers through this poem is the voice of the absent labourer, whose hook yesterday sliced the blackthorns cleanly, the voice of Lob himself.

II

A Haunted Landscape

Eleanor Farjeon recalls a letter from Edward Thomas in 1913 which describes, with a candour he himself calls 'incontinent', the nature of his dilemma:

> The point is I have got to help myself and have been steadily spoiling myself for the job for I don't know how long. I am very incontinent to say these things. If I had never said them to anyone I should have been someone else and somewhere else. You see the central evil is self-consciousness carried as far beyond selfishness as selfishness is beyond self-denial (not a very scientific comparison) and now amounting to a disease and all I have got to fight it with is the knowledge that in truth I am not the isolated self-considering brain which I have come to seem – the knowledge that I am something more, but not the belief that I can reopen the connection between the brain and the rest . . . And I keep afflicting myself by imagining all the distasteful work as if it were a great impossible mountain just ahead. Please forgive me and try not to give any thought to this flat grey shore which surprises the tide by being inaccessible to it. (*LFY,* pp. 12-13).

The image is of a nature divided against itself, paralysed by internal contradictions; and in each instance the disjunction occurs at the point of 'connection between the brain and the rest'. It seems primarily a personal dilemma; but the word 'self-consciousness' in Thomas's writings usually has a more than psychological resonance. It describes the plight of the 'superfluous man'

[59]

whose condition, in other contexts, Thomas attributed to a social aetiology. The metaphor of the sea and shore is akin to that we have seen used in *The South Country* to figure a frustrated social power, and in *The Country* to represent a London whose energy is 'in bondage'.

There are indications here too of this contrary diagnosis, consistently suppressed by a defensive shrinking which apologetically withdraws at the moment of confiding. And this is reflected in the uneasy shifting of the topographical metaphor. The self is at once hermetically sealed in its impotence and yet perpetually vulnerable to an overwhelming external world. That world, which presents one single vast obstacle to the anguishedly active self, becomes, in the same sentence, the frustrated tide of another's concern, rebuffed by a churlish, apathetic self. The metaphor combines an evasive acquiescence with an obscure, bewildered suspicion of some unnatural obstruction to the flow of reciprocity. From this impasse it is easy to go further, to perceive the dilemma as many of the poems seem to see it, as a metaphysical burden, absolute and irremediable, at the source of all the local anguishes. In poetry and prose, the primary way in which this is done is through the topos of a landscape which rebuffs and excludes a vagrant self.

In *The Isle of Wight* (1911), for example, a rather slight topographical work, the rebuff offered by a recalcitrantly alien world to the human mind is a submerged and recurrent motif. Though the book hints at more immediately social reasons for the feeling, speaking of Down dwellers not yet 'infected with the modern curse or virus of restlessness and dissatisfaction with their life . . . as if, living alone with nature on those heights . . . the contagion had not reached them', (pp. 40–41), the disease imagery more frequently relates to an apparently metaphysical condition. An eighteenth-century obelisk glimpsed on the horizon

provokes the comment, 'It looks as if it ought to mean
something, and the human mind accepts it through the
wandering eye as significant' (p. 37): 'ought' registers a
gulf between the anxious intuition of meaning and the
inability to decipher it. 'Significance' now requires an
act of faith. Mind in this book is constantly thwarted in
its attempts to find meaning in a world which at once
hints at and preserves its secrets. Thus in one place
'the sight travelled' unimpeded over 'The simple
rhythm of the scene', which 'set minds at rest and
invited them to pasture, each in its customary way, or
was beginning to do so, but was fatally interrupted by
one little thing'. The pastoral harmony is broken by
the sight of a solitary tortured yew on the horizon,
which releases the menace of the wood's 'cool impenetrable darkness' so that it swallows up the scene – as
one of the travellers comments – by imposing its
misery on the rest of the landscape (p. 27).

Reflecting on the scene, one of them recalls a fantasy
associated with a place which he never visits without 'a
story haunting my mind but never quite defining itself'. He tells of a man returning to a farm which, like a
'stupid sphinx', seems to embody 'the challenge of
matter to spirit' (pp. 34–5). The farm has stubbornly
refused to be humanized. Underneath the chatter of
sparrows and 'fowls senselessly ejaculating sybilline
things' (as with the sphinx, there is a suggestion of
esoteric meaning uttered as gibberish) he senses the
sullen vacuity at the heart of nature, kept at bay by
language, which could at any moment reassert its
ancient sway:

> If only the sparrows were to cease it would be intol-
> erable, for underneath the thin pall of their chatter he
> knew that there was a still deadlier silence which it was
> their business to gloss over, as the physician in a room
> of sickness and pain talks continually to propitiate the

awful dumb white bed and to protect himself and the waiting nurse. Heaven preserve him from that silence which would rush in like a sea if the birds were to cease. (p. 35)

Nature for Thomas is both a desolate emptiness outside mind and a flood of vital creation from which the self is excluded. The image of rain frequently combines both these aspects. *The Icknield Way* is one of Thomas's most dispirited books, written from necessity alone, but it rises on occasions to an overwrought intensity such as that which is one source for the poem 'Rain'. Here rain, as he lies awake in a strange place, 'at first . . . as pleasant . . . as it had long been desired' ceases to be 'a sweet sound and symbol' and becomes 'a majestic and finally a terrible thing', 'accusing and trying me and passing judgement' for rebellion against 'the order of nature'. Words as if spoken by 'a ghostly double' beside him begin to define his own exhaustion:

There will never be any summer any more, and I am weary of everything. I stay because I am too weak to go. I crawl on because it is easier than to stop. I put my face to the window. There is nothing out there but the blackness and the sound of rain. Neither when I shut my eyes can I see anything. I am alone. Once I heard through the rain a bird's questioning watery cry – once only and suddenly. It seemed content, and the solitary note brought up against me the order of nature, all its beauty, exuberance and everlastingness like an accusation. I am not a part of nature. I am alone. There is nothing else in my world but my dead heart and brain within me and the rain without. (pp. 280–3)

It is not difficult to deduce more practical reasons (of which the book itself is one) for this sense of exhaustion. The delinquency which seems to be a cosmic revolt rationalizes a more immediate shame. This 'ghostly double' thinks of himself as 'weak' and 'ignorant' like the unborn, 'and like the unborn I wait and wait, knowing neither what has been nor what is to come'. Yet at the same time he is a sole survivor, for 'All else has perished except me and the rain', but this apocalyptic note in turn merges with the idea of the Fall, for the rain 'chants monotonous praise of the order of nature, which I have disobeyed or slipped out of', and the 'unborn' becomes the perpetually posthumous: 'Fool! you were never alive. Lie still. Stretch out yourself like foam on a wave, and think no more of good and evil.' The rain takes on some of the same symbolic force as the elements in 'Wind and Mist' – a reification of impersonal powers which are at once indifferent and persecuting. The very passivity of the subject is the crime for which it is also punishment. The subject is doubled too, a ghost self-haunted, and haunted by a nature which is both exuberance and entropy. His vision here is one Thomas found in Lascelles Abercrombie: 'man separate from the rest of the beasts . . . the One and the Many, and the longing of created things to be unmade again' (*DC*, 29 February 1908).

In 1909, Thomas employed the metaphor he was to use to Farjeon about Jefferies who, he says, learned not despair, but hope, from such a vision of human marginality, coming to recognize 'the most tragic condition of man's greatness – his self-consciousness. If the sea waves were to be self-conscious, they would cease to wash the shore; a self-conscious world would fester and stink in a month. Many men survive the terror. Jefferies survived it' (*RJ*, p. 305). Jefferies 'has been in hell, and dreamed more terrible dreams than when de Quincey lay down with crocodiles', but, in a frequent adaptation of a favourite line in Wordsworth (*RJ*, pp. 189-90):

We make our own happiness and order, or not at all. These dreams only urge upon him yet more strongly to search for a 'soul-life' which shall be independent of Nature and the idea of deity. He has really achieved the most ancient discovery of the theologians – that man stands apart from the rest of created things. But instead of being humbled by this – of seeking for some cause such as sin – he sees in the isolation a great hope. It is man that is supreme in man's world. Let us give way to our virtues and energies, and cease to look for help apart from man.

Throughout Thomas's verse, a benign view of an entropy held back by human meanings vies with the morbidity of a putrescing universe such as he envisages here. Such a vision finds its most macabre expression in 'The Hollow Wood', with its insinuation that the hollowness represents a spiritual as well as a physical decay. As readers we find our responses continually dislocated by metaphoric shifts, similes which destabilize familiar words, carrying dis-ease and disintegration into the body of language itself:

> Out in the sun the goldfinch flits
> Along the thistle-tops, flits and twits
> Above the hollow wood
> Where birds swim like fish –
> Fish that laugh and shriek –
> To and fro, far below
> In the pale hollow wood.
>
> Lichen, ivy, and moss
> Keep evergreen the trees
> That stand half-flayed and dying,
> And the dead trees on their knees
> In dog's-mercury and moss:
> And the bright twit of the goldfinch drops
> Down there as he flits on thistle-tops.

The eerie analogies in which 'birds swim like fish – /

Fish that laugh and shriek', brings out the strange inversion and inturnedness of this scene, while the echoes of Sir James Frazer's dying god add a peculiar twist to the idea of an evergreenness produced by decomposition, just as 'pale hollow' hints at the sunken cheeks of Keats's knight, victim of 'La Belle Dame Sans Merci', and William Morris's romance 'The Hollow Land'. Yet lichen, ivy and moss are not only parasites, but life forms in their own right, so that this vision, presaging *The Waste Land,* nevertheless finds a kind of vitality festering even in decay.

The sinister quality of this is matched in Thomas's poetry only perhaps by 'Two Houses'. The first house is a farmhouse which 'smiles' on the riverside, 'Between a sunny bank and the sun', 'pleasant to look at / And remember', 'velvet-hushed and cool under the warm tiles', so that – in an image which turns on the edge of ominousness – travellers stop and 'Look down at it like a wasp at the muslined peach.' This menace is in fact developed in the picture of the second house, which 'stood there long before':

> And as if above graves
> Still the turf heaves
> Above its stones:
> Dark hangs the sycamore,
> Shadowing kennel and bones
> And the black dog that shakes his chain and moans.
> And when he barks, over the river
> Flashing fast,
> Dark echoes reply,
> And the hollow past
> Half yields the dead that never
> More than half hidden lie:
> And out they creep and back again for ever.

The 'hollow past' here gives the lie to the pastoral

vision of an England which is all beneficence and plenitude. This is a darker version of that image of the manor house founded on 'a thousand years . . . of bloody tyranny and tyranny that poisons quietly without blows' of *The South Country*. That this poem recalls that passage is indicated by the reference, in the second stanza, to the house being 'caught / Far out of reach / Of the road's dust / And the dusty thought / Of passers-by', which echoes the remark, there, that the 'harmony' of earth, sky and house 'is a thing as remote from me here in the dusty road as is the green evening sky'. The poem here rips the ideological 'surfaces' of 'harmony' away from this vision of England, to reveal that it is in reality a haunted landscape, full of ghosts and dark echoes of historic brutality and oppression, watched over by a black dog that comes straight out of old English tales of the supernatural. What is 'half-hidden', far from being the usual sought-after beauty and wholeness, is a gruesome past which manifests itself like a revenant, and the peculiar power of that last line lies in its enactment of a nightmare cycle of recurring oppression from which there seems to be no escape. The return of the repressed transfixes the passer-by in ideology as securely as the wasp is 'caught' (the word used earlier in all innocence it seemed of the house) in a wasp-trap.

The ghost is one of the commonest tropes in Thomas's poetry. His English landscapes are in fact peopled primarily by ghosts, usually associated with memory and the return of the past. 'Two Pewits', for example, share the darkened earth only with 'the ghost who wonders why / So merrily they cry and fly, / Nor choose 'twixt earth and sky'. Like Thomas, then, the ghost is between two worlds, having to choose one or the other, condemned to wander restless and dissatisfied between them. In 'It rains', nature itself, in

the figure of the parsley flower, concludes the poem
'suspended still and ghostly white, / The past hovering
as it revisits the light'. In 'The Chalk Pit', one of the
two speakers remarks that '"its emptiness and silence /
And stillness haunt me, as if just before / It was not
empty, silent, still, but full / Of life of some kind,
perhaps tragical"', and goes on:

> 'In my memory
> Again and again I see it, strangely dark,
> And vacant of a life but just withdrawn.
> We have not seen the woodman with the axe.
> Some ghost has left it now as we two came.'

What the site was once full of, in fact, is all that dead
labour which created the chalk pit in the first place,
the woodman whose axe still echoes, and those before
him who dug for chalk there. In 'House and Man', the
poet's memory of both is as dim 'As a reflection in a
rippling brook'. But if the empty-sounding house in the
woods seems haunted, its owner is the ghost, and his
ghostliness is linked automatically to an image of
poverty which hints at why the landscape is empty of
people: 'He seemed to hang rather than stand there,
half / Ghost-like, half like a beggar's rag, clean wrung /
And useless on the briar'. In 'Roads' the roads are
haunted by the ghosts of soldiers coming back from
France, who unlike the poet, 'Returning lightly dance',
freed from the burden he still carries. In 'Tears' he
even imagines ghost tears, which fall in response
to a strangely contrary vision of 'young English
countrymen, / Fair-haired and ruddy, in white tunics',
playing 'The British Grenadiers'. While in 'The Gypsy'
it is again music that summons up ghosts, making
the poet feel a posthumous man in a landscape which
is itself, in its hollow emptiness, that of Hades' fields.
The Gypsy's tune focuses the contradictions of Thomas's

England, for it peoples the emptied landscape at the moment that it reminds him of his own vagrancy, shared with the gypsies:

> That night he peopled for me the hollow wooded land,
> More dark and wild than stormiest heavens, that I
>   searched and scanned
> Like a ghost new-arrived. The gradations of the dark
> Were like an underworld of death, but for the spark
> In the Gypsy boy's black eyes as he played and stamped
>   his tune,
> 'Over the hills and far away,' and a crescent moon.

What seems to have been missed in all the talk about Thomas's ruralism is its negative aspect, this insistence on the 'hollow', unpeopled emptiness of the English countryside, what even as sunny a poem as 'Health' refers to as 'the dark hollow land'. For all their lushness, his landscapes are not totally unrelated to those 'comatose and scarcely living' terrains which were to feature in W. H. Auden's poetry. This is the landscape of rural recession, displaying, in Paul Thompson's words, 'the beauty of decay'.

Take, for example, the subtle hint in a poem as apparently personal as 'Over the Hills', with its record, again prefiguring Auden's more urgent journeyings, of a passage over 'the horizon ridge / To a new country, the path I had to find / By half-gaps that were stiles once in the hedge'. It's not only that the poet is concerned with his own unexplained vagrancy, and the obscure necessity for it. It is apparent also in those signs of a once significant human presence reverting to nature. The paths have to be found, the stiles have disappeared and become no more than half-gaps in the hedge, which itself is presumably running wild. Nobody comes here any more. This is not wild untrammelled nature, but a landscape abandoned to reversion. The harvest evening seemed 'endless'; but in a poem about recurrent endings and beginnings what strikes one is the desolation of this 'harvest' scene.

There are no people working in the fields, and the only sign of activity is 'The pack of scarlet clouds running across / The harvest evening'. In the inn which he subsequently comes to 'all were kind, / All were strangers', in a way which sets the seal on this sense of an exclusion which is necessary but not desired on either side. That hint of a wordplay on 'kind', suggesting consanguinity as 'strangers' withdraws it, indicates shyly the more tenuous, tentative relations of this newer world, and recalls the repeated antithesis of 'strange and familiar' in Thomas's poetry as attributes of all that he holds most dear, from language, through landscape, to the beloved's face. A sentence that proceeds at a leisurely narrative pace through eight and a half lines, seeming to enjoy this new beginning, is then cut short by the way in which the next sentence starts abruptly with its main clause, and foregrounds its negatives by enjambment and rhyme:

> I did not know my loss
> Till one day twelve months later suddenly
> I leaned upon my spade and saw it all,
> Though far beyond the sky-line.

This suddenness contrasts with the belatedness of the recognition. The day on which he passed the horizon ridge had come back to mind 'Often and often', but its meaning is borne home now with an abrupt shock of interruption. Significantly, it is at a natural pause in the middle of work that this recognition comes, though the poem doesn't make clear whether the work is the cause of his vagrancy or the source of the sense of loss – whether, in fact, it is welcome or imposed work, pleasure or toil. But the entry into what is thereafter 'almost a habit' of pausing to think about the lost landscape adds to the sense that this work is a burden, not freedom. Even though he is perpetually waylaid by this recall, the poem indicates it is a futile and even vexatious thing, and the subject's state of mind is hinted at by the epithet 'restless' applied to the brook, as opposed to the lost 'rest' of the lake which is its source:

> Recall
> Was vain: no more could the restless brook
> Ever turn back and climb the waterfall
> To the lake that rests and stirs not in its nook,
> As in the hollow of the collar-bone
> Under the mountain's head of rush and stone.

The poem may to some extent make a bow to Heraclitus' observations on time, that no one can bathe in the same stream twice; but its real theme is one of dispossession as the result of some undefined necessity. It is not the effortless freedom of the brook but its restlessness that sets the mood, and this is presented as its response to the *necessity* that drives water always to run downhill.

It helps to recall Thomas's appeal to W. H. Auden when we consider such a poem as 'The Mill-Water'. For the later poet's social and political sense of landscapes made desolate by deliberate human choice throws a light back on to some of Thomas's innuendoes here, and helps to rescue such a poem from being a mere vision of metaphysical gloom. It restores the poem, that is, to a tradition of social protest that reaches back to 'The Deserted Village' and forward to Auden's 'The Water-shed'. 'The Mill-Water' does not, after all, deny its economic dimension, any more than Goldsmith's poem:

> Only the sound remains
> Of the old mill;

Gone is the wheel;
On the prone roof and walls the nettle reigns.

Water that toils no more
Dangles white locks
And, falling, mocks
The music of the mill-wheel's busy roar.

This is nature released from the bondage of toil, certainly, finding its playful satisfactions in the kind of dalliance that graced earlier and less self-conscious pastoral. But such careless dangling (where 'white locks' already suggests that this is not the playfulness of Milton's 'L'Allegro' but the maundering mock-pastoral senility of a Lear) leads at once to a slimy mocking – a mere imitation of the music of work, but also a taunting of it from a position of complete and malevolent irresponsibility. It is merely 'Pretty to see', superficial, but also deceptive, concealing its real and ancient menace. By day, such 'pretty' irrelevancies seem to be no threat to either human work or an apparently equivalent 'play'. Even thought, in all its abstractness, can keep down its menace, and even empty talk contain it. But by night, such constraints are overthrown, the careful limits of consciousness, all those elaborate antitheses by which mind organizes its world (once/no more, day/night, talk/noise, labour/play, light/gloom, sound/sense, solitude/company, grief/delight, often/sometimes, drowned/climbs, begins/ends) succumb to an unbounded vagueness. Sense and thought alike are overwhelmed by it.

'Difference' itself, as a human system for ordering reality, is parodically undermined by a night which actually 'makes the difference'. It is, in fact, the un-varying, 'changelessly calling', indifference of the water which prevails over all human distinctions and hierarchies of value. Whether thought is drowned in or climbs out of, begins or ends upon this sound is a matter of complete indifference to it. 'Haunting' and 'concluding' are almost equally negative in their force. The water even mocks the human antitheses of 'solitude' and 'company' by a paradoxical companioning of opposites, of a 'silentness' and 'sound' which makes both solitude and company equally ineffectual and dispiriting:

> Pretty to see, by day
> Its sound is naught
> Compared with thought
> And talk and noise of labour and of play.
>
> Night makes the difference.
> In calm moonlight,
> Gloom infinite,
> The sound comes surging in upon the sense:
>
> Solitude, company, –
> When it is night, –
> Grief or delight
> By it must haunted or concluded be.
>
> Often the silentness
> Has but this one
> Companion;
> Wherever one creeps in the other is:
>
> Sometimes a thought is drowned
> By it, sometimes
> Out of it climbs;
> All thoughts begin or end upon this sound,
>
> Only the idle foam
> Of water falling
> Changelessly calling,
> Where once men had a work-place and a home.

Far from being merely playful, this idleness, set against the lost assurances of work and home, is actively sinister. That 'surging in upon' is an invasive violation of sense. But 'creeps', seemingly its opposite, is even more invasive in its sly insidiousness. The water is not a mere indifferent noise: it haunts, it vociferously *calls* to a suicide and surrender already hinted at in that drowning of thought, with its sly passive voice subverting all the conscious effort of climbing out, as in all those tales of water-nymphs seducing men to their doom in mill races. It invites the spirit, that is, to succumb to dereliction and defeat in the way that one human community already has. Yet at the same time it is important to stress the economic dimension here. For what has led the nettle to reign over this once busy site is the supersession and replacement of one form of production by another.

It is not the nettle, 'the challenge of matter to spirit', which is supreme. Rather, 'matter' has only been given its opportunity to mock and menace because of a change in economic circumstances. The water, after all, once had a human significance and function, was harnessed to human purposes: it toiled. If it is now reduced to a dangerous and unproductive idling, it is because human beings abandoned it. The poem, like the sense, has been invaded by a roar which seems to have disengaged itself from its material source and become a symbol of a whole hostile metaphysical order. The poem closes, however, by drawing back from the brink, to relocate that siren 'calling' as '*Only* the idle foam', stressing that it is its exclusion from human work and community that turns it into something negative and corrosive. It is not, in the end, the terror of 'nature' which overwhelms thought in this place. It is the void left by a deliberate human withdrawal from confronting 'matter' in the only terms matter responds to – those of a work which transforms the inertly given into meaning and value, overcoming entropy by turning stone and wood into house and mill and water-wheel, and releasing their dead labour in turn into the means for producing flour and bread and, ultimately, more labour power.

In that much more benign recording of a changing economic order and its supersessions, 'Tall Nettles', entropy is kept at bay by a recall of human values and discriminations, of a liking which can enjoy both dust and shower, flower and nettle, sweetness and sting. Here the incursion of and reversion to wilderness can be kept in its place, in the corner of a still productive farmyard:

> Tall nettles cover up, as they have done
> These many springs, the rusty harrow, the plough
> Long worn out, and the roller made of stone:
> Only the elm butt tops the nettles now.
>
> This corner of the farmyard I like most:
> As well as any bloom upon a flower
> I like the dust on the nettles, never lost
> Except to prove the sweetness of a shower.

'It is sometimes consoling to remember how much of the pleasantness of English country is due to men, by chance or design', Thomas observes in the essay 'Chalk Pits' (*LS*, p. 27). The landscape is shaped by and records 'The sowing of various crops, the planning of hedges and building of walls, the trimming of woods'. Yet there is always a double edge to such consolation in Thomas, for if the ubiquity of the human everywhere present in its effects testifies to survival it testifies, too, to its opposite, supersession. Continuing the ambivalent tone, Thomas adds what is part consolation and part ruefulness: 'There is no building which the country cannot digest and assimilate if left to itself in about twenty years.' A deserted London, he suggests, would be a pleasant place for this reason, not that poisonous swamp Jefferies envisaged in *After London*. This play of survival and displacement is typical of Thomas's attitude to the changing ratios of human and natural in the English countryside, expressing in miniature a larger contradiction in his work between desire for permanence and the recognition of transiency.

In 'The Barn', for example, the initial protest 'They should never have built a barn there, at all', and the idea of a degeneration, is balanced by the playful sense of a changing utility. The barn had a precise historical origin and function, built by Job Knight in 1854, but even then its human role was qualified by a further, unintended one, for, it seems, it was 'Built to keep corn for rats and men', so that if 'Now there's fowls in the roof, pigs on the floor', there is no real sense of an irreparable break between human and natural. The barn, after all, always had a role other than that men attributed to it. Even now, its very decay has a productive power: 'What thatch survives is dung for the grass, / The best grass on the farm.' Nothing is ever obsolete. Its function merely changes. There is no such thing as absolute loss in nature and, the poem concludes, now that starlings can no longer find a place to nest any more, 'It's the turn of lesser things, I suppose. / Once I fancied 'twas starlings they built it for.'

This return to the act of building at the end raises again the whole question of the discrepancy between intended and actual results, in a changing world. But the fancifulness of that suggestion has a real edge to it. In a sense, the barn *was* built for the starlings, and for rats, pigs and fowl as much as for the unknown, long dead 'they' who did the building. It is, after all, a different 'they' (though equally it seems unknown to the poet) who will cut down the elm tomorrow and leave the barn 'As I shall be left, maybe'. But this new 'they' will leave the barn because "'Twould not pay to pull down'. Quietly and surreptitiously, the poet has inserted economics into the scene. Things survive partly because they are not worth the cost of removing. By implication, he too is the same, just as, by implication, he is linked to the barn in the query 'What holds it up?' Here, again, is the shadow of the superfluous man, taking whimsical delight in his uselessness. But here, too, is that sense of a nature perpetually displacing human values and needs to the margins, making use of the labours of men and women for its own purposes, and replacing one generation of 'theys' with another in the propagation of its own alien needs.

'Women he liked' seems full of the presence of human beings. Its 'slow-climbing train' from which travellers hear the stormcock singing in the elms seems to dominate the landscape. The elms themselves testify to that presence, for long ago Farmer Hayward planted them out of love. But it is in this very act, in this love, that the displacement of the human begins. The man himself is an ambiguous patriarch, at once an earth spirit, liking women and loving horses, altering the landscape by his acts, and, at the same time, an unintentionally negative force, for the trees he planted have turned the lane where nightingales once sang into slough and gloom, fit only for the stormcock. There is an omen here of an England changing for the worse, as a result of acts which are intended to be beneficial but actually destroy.

The poem itself enacts the displacements and evasiveness of the reality it describes. It starts by foregrounding the carnality of its creative patriarch, but this is displaced at once by a higher priority, as love takes precedence over liking:

[76]

> Women he liked, did shovel-bearded Bob,
> Old Farmer Hayward of the Heath, but he
> Loved horses. He himself was like a cob,
> And leather-coloured. Also he loved a tree.
>
> For the life in them he loved most living things,
> But a tree chiefly. All along the lane
> He planted elms where now the stormcock sings
> That travellers hear from the slow-climbing train.

But if the enjambment on 'but he' reinforces that shift, the apparent afterthought 'Also he loved a tree' unsettles us further before we have settled into that comparison between man and horse. It seems that the poem is about to move away again into a generalizing dimension, but we are jerked back from this by that curt reiteration, 'But a tree chiefly'. The second stanza then seems to find its feet in the story of Bob's planting of the trees, and though the stormcock and the travelling seem to point off in a new direction, they don't at this moment distract from the apparently untrammelled achievement of Bob's act. The shift now, however, is from material to spiritual appropriation of the landscape, that naming which, in turning a track into a lane, seems to foreground human lordship over nature:

> Till then the track had never had a name
> For all its thicket and the nightingales
> That should have earned it. No one was to blame.
> To name a thing beloved man sometimes fails.

It is only in retrospect that the shift from nightingales to stormcock becomes an omen of an England itself moving from calm to turbulence, for if the nightingales sing of beauty and love, the stormcocks presage human as well as natural upheaval. In June 1916, when this poem was written, the slough and gloom of a lane which was once named and claimed by no one, could not but call up the desolation of another No Man's Land, in Flanders. Bob's love and labours have not reclaimed the landscape; rather they have turned 'a thing beloved' into something else, alien and negative. The lane has acquired Bob's name not in celebration of his memory, but in reproach and blame. The dénouement turns the tables on both us and Bob, turning that 'no one' who was to blame into a name that carries odium, in a place where now no one passes:

> Many years since, Bob Hayward died, and now
> None passes there because the mist and the rain
> Out of the elms have turned the lane to slough
> And gloom, the name alone survives, Bob's Lane.

Displacement is the key to this poem, built into its very narrative structure. Bob is abruptly dismissed in a brief epitaph. Other human passers-by are likewise dismissed, in that negative pronoun. In the end, it is the stormcock which inherits. The poem has repeatedly teased us with a series of possible themes: is it about women and Bob, Bob himself, Bob and horses, Bob and trees, the travellers, the lane, the birds, the acts of planting or of naming? In the end, however, it is not primarily even about naming a lane. Human acts and intentions are both alike displaced by their con- sequences, taken up into an order of fatality which ironically disposes of all their illusions of authority and authorship. Love can destroy that which it wishes to serve, celebrate and enhance. We survive not in masterful appropriation of the world, but as contingent causes, displaced in our very acts of love by processes over which we have little control. Bob is reduced to a mere posthumous name, a ghostly trace of his carnal self, marginalized; but so is the lane, something only glimpsed now from the passing train, no longer a regular human thoroughfare. This poem is not the celebration of a countryman's 'indissoluble . . . organic relationship with landscape' which Edna Longley finds it (*PLP,* p. 357). It is a powerful little myth of degeneration and waste, of a countryside in decay.

The necessity which imposes decline upon a landscape is everywhere present without being specified in Thomas's poetry. It is intimately linked with that displacement and marginalization of the self which finds it hovering in ghostlike dependency on a world which seems both strange and familiar to it, from which it is excluded yet to which it feels it belongs. But a further consequence of this estrangement is that the world itself, when he tries to grasp it, seems to slip beyond his reach, become almost an imaginary terrain, inaccessible and remote, like 'The Unknown Bird', which calls 'seemingly far off – / As if a cock crowed past the edge of the world, / As if the bird or I were in a dream'. Telling the naturalists does not help, for 'neither had they heard / Anything like the notes that did so haunt me'. The haunted listener shares in the volatility and evanescence of the haunter, himself apparently moving beyond the edge of the world.

A lost Eden becomes an inevitable symbol of such estrangement, in Thomas's prose, but it is significant how even here the social aetiology of such a mood is hinted at. The image occurs several times in *Rose Acre Papers* for example:

> On every side rose and fell leagues of untenanted lawn, of a cold green, that in the light of a February dawn, so clear, so absolutely clear, looked as the savannah of Eden must have looked on that first day of the world. (p.75 ff)

The significant word is 'untenanted', as 'deserted' is in the following passage:

> Fallen leaves and fruit, gold and silver, like sheddings

from Hesperidean gardens . . . The grey and silent
landscape of few trees and many houses seemed a
deserted camp . . . or a Canaan from which the happy
savage, childhood, has been vanquished. (p. 58 ff)

Estrangement enters into the very act of perception,
as in *The South Country,* where distance alone invests
the remote landscape with inexplicable significance, so
that a ridge of the downs, transfigured with golden
light, makes those 'in the valley sigh at the thought
that where we have often trod is heaven now'. But the
link between spatial and temporal distance is subjec-
tively supplied, and draws directly on personal nostalgia, for 'Such beauties of the earth, seen at a distance
and inaccessibly serene, always recall the equally inaccessible happiness of childhood. Why have we such a
melting mood for what we cannot reach?' (p. 132). The
answer lies in that social aetiology hinted at in
'Leaving Town', the opening section of *The Heart of
England,* where the narrator returns to childhood
haunts now overwhelmed by suburbia:

Nor at the end of my journey was the problem solved. It
was a land of new streets and half-built streets and
devastated lanes. Ivied elm trunks lay about with
scaffold poles, uprooted shrubs were mingled with
bricks, mortar with turf, shining baths and sinks and
rusty fire grates with dead thistles and thorns . . . An
artist who wished to depict the Fall and some sympathy
with it in the face of a ruined Eden might have had
little to do but copy an acre of the surviving fields. A
north wind . . . drove workmen and passers-by to . . .
'The King's Head', and there the medley of the land was
repeated. Irish and Cockney accents mingled with
Kentish; American would not have been out of place.
(p. 3 ff)

In 'Lob', the old man had spoken to the poet of a
footpath now out of use to such an extent that only his

[80]

seasoned eye can still read its human meaning. Not only is the path sunk into dereliction. It also seems to be closed off as private property, which all but the daring traveller will be wary of trespassing upon. If Lob's 'home was where he was free' in a land everywhere parcelled up by fences and 'No Trespassing' signs and the new suburban sprawl, this perhaps explains why he is a wanderer, why he is so hard to get hold of, and why he is 'One of the lords of No Man's Land'. Before its Great War usage, this phrase had referred to that unclaimed land between road and hedge where tramps and gypsies set up home. At the same time, it is not difficult to see No Man's Land as a kind of 'underworld of death' like that through which the poet passes in 'The Gypsy', or like that past which is 'a strange land, most strange', in 'Parting', where 'Men of all kinds as equals range / The soundless fields and streets'. The village where he first encountered Lob can't be found again, mysteriously disappearing like the otherworldly realm of the Sidhe in Yeats's Irish folklore. Similarly, Lob is close to the tramp and poacher 'old Jack Noman' who also suddenly 'disappeared' in the last line of 'May the Twenty-third' (in an earlier draft, he dies). He is as ungraspable as a wraith.

The villages and farms of Lob's England, 'Lurking to one side up the paths and lanes, / Seldom well seen except by aeroplanes' may seem safely secluded from the encroachment of the urban world, but those overflying aeroplanes suggest an end to their security, just as 'Ages ago the road / Approached'. This encroachment is a historic process. Though 'The people stood and looked and turned, / Nor asked it to come nearer, nor yet learned / To move out there and dwell in all men's dust', this defiance is not as absolute as it seems. The man who speaks to Thomas of Lob may at the end deny that Lob is 'dead before his hour'. He may himself seem, in his departure, 'of old Jack's blood', refusing to 'remove my house out of the lane / On to the road'. He may insist that Lob 'never will admit he is dead / Till millers cease to grind men's bones for bread'. But that word 'admit' itself admits to more than it realizes, suggesting that the defiance is really the posthumous bravado of a ghost refusing his own mortality. In this light the fact that he 'disappeared / In hazel and thorn tangled with old-man's-beard' takes on a supernatural tinge, and the intangibility and evasiveness of Lob become the figure of a larger loss. This spirit of England is already no more than an image within the brain, an illusory site for all that the wandering subject feels dispossessed of.

The ghostliness of Lob thus links him with such imaginary earth-spirits as 'Lob-lie-by-the-fire', Herne the Hunter and Hob (an old name for the devil). But at the same time, that nebulously legendary figure, Robin Hood, acts as an intermediary between myth and history. For if Robin Hood is on the one hand associated with pagan spirits of the greenwood like Robin Goodfellow, he is on the other linked with a hard political history of medieval outlaws seeking asylum from unjust laws in the No Man's Land of the forest. The name of Jack Cade is thus not gratuitously called up in this list, suggesting a peasantry in revolt against its landlords, and these echoes of medieval jacqueries are extended in the closing roll call of battles, which at first seems designed merely to add a spurious nationalistic glamour to the idea of cultural continuity, but which is in fact full of ambivalence. Lob, we are told '"Although he was seen dying at Waterloo, / Hastings, Agincourt, and Sedgemoor too, – / Lives yet"'. It is not only that this is an eclectic bunch of victories and defeats for the English yeomanry. It is also that some

of them share in the very duplicity of that 'seen dying/
Lives yet' antithesis. Waterloo, supposedly a victory,
takes on a quite different significance when it is linked
with Sedgemoor, as it was by the Whig historian G. M.
Trevelyan in his immensely popular *England under
the Stuarts* in 1904. At Sedgemoor, in 1685, the West
Country peasants who had flocked to support the
pretender Monmouth's revolt against James II were
wiped out in large numbers. Their insurrection had
been brought about by an economic and social collapse
beyond their capacity to understand, but linked, by
Trevelyan, with a Waterloo which in assuring British
global hegemony, spelt the end for English agriculture:

> As the march of the man from Elba through the valleys
> of Dauphiné, so the march of King Monmouth through
> the lanes of Somerset is to the historian full of social as
> well as political significance. The record of this brief
> campaign is as the lifting of a curtain; behind it we can
> see for a moment into the old peasant life, since passed
> away into the streets and factories, suffering city-
> change. In that one glance we see, not rustic torpor, but
> faith, idealism, vigour, love of liberty and scorn of
> death. Were the yeomen and farm servants in other
> parts of England like these men of Somerset, or were
> they everywhere else of a lower type? The curtain falls;
> and knowledge is hidden forever.
> One thing is certain, that only in an age when the
> class of freehold yeomen formed a large proportion of
> the population, and employed a part at least of the
> hired labour, could any district have thus risen in arms
> against the will of the squires. The land of England was
> not then owned by the few. (ch. xii)

Trevelyan's relevance to the contemporary debate
about land ownership would hardly need spelling out
for someone like Thomas, trained as a historian and
raised in the Whig interpretation of history, as he

recorded in *The Childhood*. It is precisely in this passing away of the old life, 'suffering city-change' that, in Richard Jefferies' mechanics on the Great Western Railway and the working men and women of South Wales in 'Mothers and Sons', he had seen the hope, not only of survival but also of renewal, that phoenix rebirth of England. It is not surprising, then, that Thomas's ghost motif should also share in this duplicity. This can be seen by comparing three of the poems in which he envisages himself as a kind of revenant, a posthumous man returning to a world from which he has been expelled, but for which he still feels the tug of affiliation.

In 'Aspens', the ghostly whisper of the trees at the crossroads calls up the ghosts of a once populous landscape now emptied of its inhabitants: 'And over lightless pane and footless road, / Empty as sky, with every other sound / Not ceasing, calls their ghosts from their abode, / A silent smithy, a silent inn', turning the crossroads to 'a ghostly room' – a thoroughfare now fallen into dereliction. It is then with such necromantic powers that the poet equates his own poetic mysteries, which can be seen as an imposed necessity rather than freedom, and which carry a sense of redundancy like that threatening the blacksmith, the crossroads, and the trees.

> Over all sorts of weather, men, and times,
> Aspens must shake their leaves and men may hear
> But need not listen, more than to my rhymes.
>
> Whatever wind blows, while they and I have leaves
> We cannot other than an aspen be
> That ceaselessly, unreasonably grieves,
> Or so men think who like a different tree.

The poem, however, manages to rescue an affirmation from this sense of supersession, that last line half dismissing in turn, but diffidently, the attitudes which dismiss him and his trees. The ambivalence is everything in this mood. In 'The Ash Grove' even moments of triumph, when he seems briefly to have come home, to have found 'What most I desired, without search or desert or cost', are still darkened by the shadow of dispossession. But then in 'Good-night' triumph is snatched from the very moment of loss, the city streets reclaimed as they deepen the itinerant self's alienation. 'The Ash Grove' opens with the grove's trees half dead, and whatever human habitation they may once have sheltered erased from evidence: 'If they led to a house, long before they had seen its fall'. If he considers himself in this welcome and gladness 'without cause' to be momentarily free from the Furies, they still thrust themselves, in their very absence, into the text: 'Not even the spirits of memory and fear with restless wing, / Could climb down to molest me over the wall / That I passed through at either end without noticing'. They are there, in the same way that human traces are there, none the less monitory for not being noticed. The poet's gladness, then, is a chimerical thing, as his own identity seems already posthumous, like those effaced predecessors now confirmed to have once dwelt there. The ghostliness of this experience is compounded by the fact that it is only a memory, subject therefore to the restless spirit of memory earlier denied, a restlessness which corresponds to his own, now having travelled 'far from those hills', expelled from the momentary tranquillity:

And now an ash grove far from those hills can bring
The same tranquillity in which I wander a ghost
With a ghostly gladness, as if I heard a girl sing

The song of the Ash Grove soft as love uncrossed
And then in a crowd or in distance it were lost,

> But the moment unveiled something unwilling to die
> And I had what I most desired, without search or desert
>   or cost.

'Unwilling' is clearly not the same as 'refusing to': the very defiance reveals a deeper weakness and vulnerability. Distance has dispossessed him of the very moment in which he found that illusory fulfilment of desire, and his own death joins the succession of deaths the poem records, as the moment itself dies as another moment is born from it.

This 'ghostly gladness', however, recalls a similar moment of transit and welcome in 'Good-Night', a poem written a year earlier. The poem opens not with the characteristic flight *from* the urban landscape, but entry *into* it:

> The skylarks are far behind that sang over the down;
> I can hear no more those suburb nightingales;
> Thrushes and blackbirds sing in the gardens of the town
> In vain: the noise of man, beast, and machine prevails.

> But the call of children in the unfamiliar streets
> That echo with a familiar twilight echoing,
> Sweet as the voice of nightingale or lark, completes
> A magic of strange welcome, so that I seem a king

> Among man, beast, machine, bird, child, and the ghost
> That in the echo lives and with the echo dies.
> The friendless town is friendly; homeless, I am not lost;
> Though I know none of these doors, and meet but
>   strangers' eyes.

> Never again, perhaps, after tomorrow, shall
> I see these homely streets, these church windows alight,
> Not a man or woman or child among them all:
> But it is All Friends' Night, a traveller's good night.

The sequence of bird songs as he makes this journey into the heart of darkness succumbs, finally, to 'noise'.

But this noise is in turn transmuted back into meaningful sound, 'the call of children', calling up echoes which retain enough human resonance to make the unfamiliar familiar again, so that it acquires the sweetness of the birds, and is restored to a meaningful 'voice'. That this is a real transformation is indicated by the word 'magic', as well as by that oxymoronic 'strange welcome', evoking Thomas's repeated linking of 'strange' and 'familiar' as a way of expressing the looser bonds of a modern urban society.

At the end of the final line of one stanza the poet is suspended, seemingly a king. At the end of the first line of the next he is reduced, in this suspension, to a ghost, doubly suspended in that moment between times, as the repetition of the word 'echo' itself enacts its shortlived echoic effect. Repetition of key words through the poem in fact tries to achieve that reconciliation of familiar and strange which is its theme. The words return to us in their echoing, taking on new meanings as they remind us of old ones, as 'unfamiliar' returns tamed into 'familiar', and 'echo' (present tense of the verb) as 'echoing' (present participle turned into noun), as 'friendless' becomes 'friendly' and 'strange' becomes 'strangers'. Similarly, the negative list 'man, beast, and machine' of the opening stanza acquires the bird and child of the first two stanzas in a way which domesticates even the strangeness of the 'ghost'. This self may be evanescent, vulnerable, at risk, but it is also a revenant returning home, welcomed back, as the invented festal day 'All Friends' Night' both calls up and alters, makes familiar and consoling, the mystery and menace of All Souls' Night, when the dead return. The 'homeless' subject finds his place in the 'homely' streets. All these negative constructions of perception, 'I can hear no more', 'I know none', 'Never again . . . shall I see', are redeemed from loss: 'I am not lost'.

Constructions which end in '-less' are transformed into their opposites. The last word of the poem catches this strange/familiar duality, for of course 'good-night' is both farewell and greeting, spoken by the traveller as he departs and spoken to him as he passes. The very language of the poem effects the completion of which it speaks, 'completes / A magic of strange welcome', taking the lost soul of the travelling ghost back into a community of language, of mutual exchanges which redeem the self from volatility.

This is one of the most affirmative of Thomas's poems about the relation between individual and society, redeeming even his own ghostly evanescence. The last two lines of stanza three in rhythm and reference call up another ghost, an intertextual echo which hints at what Thomas is rejecting here: the mood of Hardy's 'Wessex Heights', which finds liberty only in a voluntary estrangement of the self from society:

> In the towns I am tracked by phantoms having weird
>   detective ways—
> Shadows of beings who fellowed with myself in earlier
>   days:
> They hang about at places, and they say harsh heavy
>   things—
> Men with a wintry sneer, and women with tart
>   disparagings.

Hardy's poem ends with the speaker seeking refuge from ghostly others in the solitude of the heights. 'Where men have never cared to haunt, nor women have walked with me, / And ghosts then keep their distance; and I know some liberty.' By contrast, Thomas sees himself as the ghost who is welcomed back from solitude into the homely arms of the towns. That they are as transient in his life as he in theirs seems to make no difference. The reconciliation has occurred that turns noise into meaningful sound, into greeting and call and welcome.

In 'Home' Thomas records another brief moment of return, an All Friends' Night on which the traveller, like a revenant, comes back 'somehow from somewhere far'. The very vagueness of those adverbs suggests how real and tangible by contrast is something as insubstantial as the April mist. The welcome this time is from a rural landscape, and the nationality he recovers is in that 'immeasurable commonwealth of various life in which we have yet to learn our offices' *(RJ,* p. 156). But there is here, as in 'Good-night', the same interplay of strangeness and familiarity, the same sense of a shared language and meanings. What links the two landscapes, urban and rural, in a common comfort, however, is that which rounds off the silence as it rounds off the poem: the sound of human labour:

> Often I had gone this way before:
> But now it seemed I never could be
> And never had been anywhere else;
> 'Twas home; one nationality
> We had, I and the birds that sang,
> One memory.
>
> They welcomed me. I had come back
> That eve somehow from somewhere far:
> The April mist, the chill, the calm,
> Meant the same thing familiar
> And pleasant to us, and strange too,
> Yet with no bar.
>
> . . .
>
> Then past his dark white cottage front
> A labourer went along, his tread
> Slow, half with weariness, half with ease;
> And, through the silence, from his shed
> The sound of sawing rounded all
> That silence said.

If silence speaks, it is no longer a threat to the isolated self, but is rendered harmless, even comforting, by a community of labour within which solidarity can be rediscovered. Like the superfluous man in 'A Return to Nature', Thomas finds his return home here in solidarity with a class which *has* built, finds, too, that there is at last no bar between himself and his past and himself and the future. That self-consciousness of which he wrote to Farjeon, which he saw Jefferies struggling with, is overcome by the kind of practical, sensuous engagement with the material world that the sound of sawing and the weariness and ease of the labourer alike imply. As he wrote in *The South Country:*

> [S]ome men, particularly sailors and field labourers, but also navvies and others who work heavily with their hands, have this glory of use. Their faces, their clothes, their natures all appear to act and speak harmoniously, so that they cause a strong impression of personality which is to be deeply enjoyed in a world of masks, especially of black clerical masks. (p. 183)

Nostalgically visiting a Welsh village he had known as a child, in *Beautiful Wales,* Thomas is initially angered to find workmen demolishing a house which had once seemed to him a symbol of the 'life contemplative' of a leisurely intelligentsia, but which also in its garden preserved remnants of an even older order:

> In one corner . . . had been a tangle of elder and bramble, which (so we used to fancy) might possibly have – by pure and unbroken descent, miraculously escaping all change – the sap of Eden in their veins.

But such dreams of escaping change are seductive illusions. The inhabitants of this squalid, semi-industrialized village, subjected to all the strains of transition from rural to urban, have been forced to cope with it, and his final response is one of admiration for the workmen: 'I liked them for the complete lack of self-consciousness which allowed them to expose quite fearlessly their angular figures' (pp. 114-5). Aurelius the superfluous man in *The Happy-Go-Lucky Morgans* believes the future to lie with such men, because only they have the energy which, if unfettered, could liberate such rootless vagrants as himself from their ghostly morbidity. In the turbulent political climate of the pre-war decade, such an exalted and democratic optimism must have seemed not improbably far from fulfilment:

> He came to believe that, lacking as their life might be in familiar forms of beauty and power, it possessed, nevertheless, a profound unconsciousness and dark strength which might some day bring forth beauty . . . and had already given them a fitness to their place which he had for no place on earth. (p. 99)

III

The Breeding of a Mystery

The place of mind in nature is one of Thomas's pre-occupations. But whereas in the poetry it is all implicit, embodied in particular moments of perception and experience, in the prose he repeatedly speculates on the significance of such moments, trying to tease a meaning out of them. His study of Richard Jefferies is particularly rich in such speculations, for Jefferies' own mysticism had placed the question on the agenda. Convinced that 'there is no god in nature' and that 'by no course of reasoning, however tortuous, can nature and the universe be fitted to the mind', Jefferies nevertheless persisted in the attempt to probe the riddle of consciousness. Throughout his life, Thomas noted, he was preoccupied with the struggle to understand those '"indefinable aspirations [which] filled him"' as a result of his intense moments of oneness with nature on the downs'. From the age of eighteen he sought the '"inner and esoteric meaning"' of those sensations which 'began to come at him "from all the visible universe"'. But initially, Thomas says, 'the mood, the very vocabulary, of these early country books was against the revelation of which he was in search'. It was only by turning away from 'lonely ecstasy in the downs' to seek one which 'will distribute the same force and balm among the cities of men below' that Jefferies found his answer, not 'an unsocial virtue, but . . . one that touches all men; his aim the ultimate one of joy'. It is in the same terms that

Thomas too sought a language in which to understand and restore value to those 'brief momentary ravishments of daily life' which constitute such a large part of his poetry (*RJ* ch. xiii, *passim*).

Thomas was himself sufficiently 'that not uncommon type, strict agnostic and evolutionist' (*DC*, 27 June 1911) to find any supernatural explanation of mind unacceptable. At the same time, his father's positivism had immunized him against mechanical and behaviouristic interpretations of consciousness. In the 'Pragmatism' of the American psychologist William James (1842–1910), the brother of Henry James, he found, along with many of his generation, a philosophy of mind which spoke to his own needs. For James sought to ground the subjective, insubstantial stuff of consciousness, what he called 'ideality', within the objective, material body of reality, without reducing the one to the other. He sought, that is, a ratio between mind and matter which succumbed neither to the delusion of grandeur which leads the man in 'Wind and Mist' to think he has created the downs, nor to the abject surrender of human freedom into which he shrinks when the chaos of the material world surges vengefully back. There is no consistency in the man's emotional response to the landscape, which veers between astonishment, pride, terror and contempt. A major part of James's attraction for Thomas is that he tried to find some consistent ground upon which to found epistemological value and significance. And he sought a clue to the way ordinary daily consciousness construed its meanings by investigating those abnormal 'momentary ravishments' which form such a large part of the spiritual repertoire of Thomas's age.

This project was summed up in the immensely popular work *The Varieties of Religious Experience*, which went through several editions in the years immediately after its publication in 1902. Thomas found in James an explanation of consciousness which reopened the connection between the 'isolate self-considering brain' and the rest, which restored to the living texture of experience, the changing moods and complex evanescent feelings of the individual, a reality and an importance denied to it by contemporary science. Central to this concern is the idea of *value*. Thomas's poetry continually frets over how to justify those inward and shifting states, and how to vindicate the faith that things out there, in the external world, have an intrinsic worth. Such a question, as we shall see, cannot for Thomas be detached from his vision of England.

One such observation of James's Thomas quotes in his introduction to Jefferies' *The Hills and the Vale* (1909) to explain Jefferies' own nature-mysticism:

> Professor William James, in 'Varieties of Religious Experience', describes four marks by which states of mind may be recognized as mystical. The subject says that they defy expression. They are 'states of insight into depths of truth unplumbed by the discursive intellect . . . and, as a rule, they carry with them a curious sense of authority for aftertime', because the mystic believes that 'we both become one with the Absolute, and we become aware of our oneness'. (p. xxvi)

For James, such states were obscure momentary intuitions by the subject of his real integration with the 'objective' universe he inhabits and, in perceiving, recreates, and offered considerable clues to the under-standing of quotidian consciousness. In *The Country* (pp. 26–7), Thomas cites a passage from James's *Talks to Students on Some of Life's Ideals* (published in 1899 and frequently reprinted throughout the following decade) in which James discusses Jefferies' mystical experiences. James's comment on one such experience offered Thomas a distinction which, I shall argue, is crucial for understanding his own ideas:

Surely a worthless hour of life, when measured by the usual standards of commercial value. Yet in what other *kind* of value can the preciousness of any hour, made precious by any standard, consist, if it consist not in feelings of excited significance like these, engendered in some one, by what the hour contains?

The question of value and significance raised here lies at the heart of Thomas's own explorations, in poetry and prose, of such tenuous and evanescent states of mind. He points out that James goes on, in this chapter, to discuss W. H. Hudson's account of one 'state . . . of suspense and watchfulness' in which there was 'something between me and my intellect', and he notes that James was sorry for anyone who had not enjoyed 'this mysterious sensorial life'. For James, the devaluation of such experience arises from that gap between self and self which makes us blind to the reality of another's inner life (the chapter is itself called 'On a Certain Blindness in Human Beings'). But such a necessary estrangement he sees compounded by 'the usual standards of commercial value' which almost make it 'necessary to become worthless as a practical being, if one is to hope to attain to any breadth of insight into the impersonal world of worths as such, to have any perception of life's meaning on a large objective scale'. The intensification of subjectivity paradoxically opens up such vistas into the heart of things. James's formulation of this gulf in being recalls Thomas's poem 'Old Man', where a father is confronted by the impenetrable otherness of his own child's experience:

For the spectator, such hours . . . form a mere tale of emptiness, in which nothing happens, nothing is gained, and there is nothing to describe. They are meaningless and vacant tracts of time. To him who feels their inner

[95]

secret, they tingle with an importance that unutterably vouches for itself . . . Hands off: neither the whole of truth nor the whole of good is revealed to any single observer, although each observer gains a partial superiority of insight from the peculiar position in which he stands. (*Talks*, pp. 263–4)

Only from within the shifting moment is the world transfigured with value and significance. The spectator fails to grasp, in his insulation from the sensuous-practical experience of the observed, what James calls the 'ideality' of the subject-world he sees simply as objective behaviour. It is for just such a 'spectatorial position', accounting for 'the increasing abstractness of his style', that Thomas criticized Hardy in the *Saturday Review* (17 June 1911).

Hardy's narrative irony, Thomas suggests, 'establishes Mr Hardy as the chief character in his novels, a "weird archimage" sitting alone, "Plotting dark spells and devilish enginery", and enjoying it after his fashion', and, 'If men and women are performing for the entertainment of a god, Mr Hardy has a seat'. What he principally objects to is Hardy's narratorial 'fore-knowledge': in proleptically warning us that a word or act will turn out to have quite different consequences from the intended ones, 'he flushes to anticipate some far-off event and loses much to gain a tenuous irony'.

This contrasts directly with the kind of play with 'foreknowledge' that Thomas makes in a poem such as 'Fifty Faggots':

There they stand, on their ends, the fifty faggots
That once were underwood of hazel and ash
In Jenny Pinks's Copse. Now, by the hedge
Close packed, they make a thicket fancy alone
Can creep through with the mouse and wren. Next Spring
A blackbird or a robin will nest there,
Accustomed to them, thinking they will remain

Whatever is for ever to a bird:
This Spring it is too late; the swift has come.
'Twas a hot day for carrying them up:
Better they will never warm me, though they must
Light several Winters' fires. Before they are done
The war will have ended, many other things
Have ended, maybe, that I can no more
Foresee or more control than robin and wren.

The speaker here occupies no privileged position outside
the narrative. Rather he is situated within it, aware
that he shares this situation with other creatures, each
of which has its own different priorities and perceptions.
These creatures live in time, but have no real knowledge of it. They not only assume that the present
continues for ever into the future; they also presume
that things have always been the same in the past –
they are accustomed to the faggots as if they were a
permanent feature of the landscape, unaware of their
transiency. His knowledge is more accurate – he knows
that they were only recently underwood, knows that it
was his own sweated labour that converted them into
their present state, knows that in several winters' time
they will be gone. He can speculate, too, on the succession of creatures that may pass through the habitat he
has just created: now mouse and wren, next spring
blackbird or robin, just as he can be confident, in his
knowledge of the seasonal pattern of migrations, that
it is too late for them to nest there now. He can also,
living in time, contrast the heat of one day's work, just
past, with the heat of several winters' fires yet to come.

But just as it is only in fancy that he can creep
through the pile, so when he comes to think of the more
pressing face of the future he is as powerless as them,
but unlike them he knows of his ignorance and powerlessness, and the very vagueness of that 'many other
things' indicates how little he can pin down that future.

Written in May 1915, two months before his final decision to enlist, one of those 'many other things' which may have ended could be his own life. Yet unlike Hardy's characters, he is no mere passive victim of events. He can, within certain limits, affect his environment. He has, after all, converted underwood into faggots, created an artificial 'thicket' which will alter the creatures' lives; he has warmed himself today and stocked up heat for the future. Not only the present but that future, then, is different for these acts of will, and the play between indicative and subjunctive, as so often in his poetry, touches on this delicate balance between the openness of the future and its predetermination: fancy *can* creep, one bird or another *will* nest there; the faggots *must* light fires; the war *will* have ended, other things *may* have ended.

Foreseeing and controlling are not the absolute prerogatives of an abstracted spectator, like Hardy's President of the Immortals; they are the always provisional and speculative acts of mortals who can partially cater for the future, by their modest acts of volition and work. In contrast to a poetry like Hardy's, in which the characters, 'valuable as they are in the weaving of his patterns of density, in themselves concern him little' (*Saturday Review*), Thomas's poetry conforms to James's axiom in *The Varieties of Religious Experience* that 'the axis of reality runs solely through the egotistic places'. Thomas himself gave a name to such an approach when, in a review of W. H. Davies in 1905, he spoke of him as 'a poet of experience' (*DC*, 21 October 1905).

Thomas's own poetry is a perfect distillation of this method. 'It rains', for example, 'makes us rather sharers in a process than witnesses of a result' (*Bookman*, April 1913). The poem catches the mind in the act of groping for its experience, turning and returning in an attempt

[98]

to understand it. The opening words involve the reader at once in an immediate present of particular experience; yet the poet's personality does not intrude itself. In fact, the whole first stanza seems to insist, gently, on the absence of a subject:

> It rains, and nothing stirs within the fence
> Anywhere through the orchard's untrodden, dense
> Forest of parsley. The great diamonds
> Of rain on the grassblades there is none to break,
> Or the fallen petals further down to shake.
>
> And I am nearly as happy as possible
> To search the wilderness in vain though well,
> To think of two walking, kissing there,
> Drenched, yet forgetting the kisses of the rain:
> Sad, too, to think that never, never again,
>
> Unless alone, so happy shall I walk
> In the rain. When I turn away, on its fine stalk
> Twilight has fined to naught, the parsley flower
> Figures, suspended still and ghostly white,
> The past hovering as it revisits the light.

The separation of observer from observed, of the speaker from what is 'within the fence', is only apparent, for the mind is felt in the quality and the selection of perceptions which constitute the seemingly 'objective' description. It is the mind which moves in from the general 'It rains' to its particular aspects, 'The great diamonds/Of rain'; and it is the mind which, almost unconsciously, introduces the analogic relationship of 'rain' and 'diamond', 'forest' and 'parsley'. Human presence is implicit in this capacity to establish relations which transcend the actual.

Looking at the stanza again, we see that it is a whole complex of negatives, not a mere transcription of 'actuality'. What is there is defined in terms of what is not – 'nothing stirs . . ./Anywhere', 'untrodden', 'there is none to break', just as, later, the poet is defined by the absence of the loved one or all those other absences implicit in the qualification 'Unless alone'. A large number of Thomas's poems open thus, with a negative construction in the first sentence which inserts absence right into the heart of an achieved and actual world. The effect here is to carry the eye over the full stop which rounds off the stanza, so that the mind which is the source of negation emerges naturally out of this 'objective' scene as a defined 'I', separate from the reality it perceives, yet actively related to it through that coordinating 'And . . .'

Mind is free to explore its own limits, qualifying itself with a sense of the unachieved yet possible ('nearly as happy as possible') and impossible future ('never again', 'in vain though well'). The clausal structure of the poem enacts this volatility. The narrative impulsion is complicated by contrary movements, as associations lead into reminiscence and expectation, and the tenses fluctuate in an emotive, atemporal sequence. The poet is not overwhelmed by the waste sad time before and after, because he never abandons hold of the vital moment, in which memories and prospects are recaptured and transformed by their contact with the actual. He is thus free to turn away at the end of the poem into his own immediate future, in which nature is still vested with symbolic value. The parsley is 'suspended' because its stalk is invisible; but its apparent hovering (emphasized by the isolation of the verb at the line turning, at the midpoint of a complex sentence, between two sets of defining clauses) 'figures' the paradox of temporality itself. Unseen, its filaments reach down into the past in which it is rooted. It is suspended at once in time and space, as the poet, turning away, moves towards a future posited within the poem, yet forever held in suspense. The three stanzas define a moment, but they also project a whole life backwards and forwards in time. As Thomas observed of one of Hardy's poems in 1909, 'The moment is full of years, and it is an implied narrative' (*MP*, 9 December 1909).

This is that 'transparent' style Thomas praised in W. H. Hudson, where 'We feel that we are in contact not simply with a man's mind or his fancy, or his eyes, or his book of synonyms, but with a man . . .; the writing gives us a sense of the actual bodily presence of a man'. (*DC*, 3 June 1908). Such a sense is, in James's usage, pragmatic, presenting a presence registered through its effects on and reactions to the landscape through which it moves. The poem stresses this through imagery which, even when negative, suggests the tactile and kinetic – modes of *bodily* awareness – 'stirs . . . untrodden . . . dense . . . break . . . shake . . . drenched . . . turn away . . . fined . . . figures, suspended . . . hovering'. The eye too is engaged in an active searching – it moves with the body – and we share throughout the poem in the enacted rhythm of this search, so that the final 'hovering' is not only seen but *felt*.

In Thomas's poetry, the landscape is no mere canvas against which to parade a self-contained passion, but a three-dimensional space into which the speaker moves, which adapts to his motions, offering new perspectives and prospects as he moves through it. In 'The Barn and the Down' what the eye sees alters with the walker's location:

> It stood in the sunset sky
> Like the straight-backed down,
> Many a time – the barn
> At the edge of the town,

> So huge and dark that it seemed
> It was the hill
> Till the gable's precipice proved
> It impossible.
>
> Then the great down in the west
> Grew into sight,
> A barn stored full to the ridge
> With black of night;
>
> And the barn fell to a barn
> Or even less
> Before critical eyes and its own
> Late mightiness.

The alternations of dimension and significance – the down growing, the barn shrinking – are functions of the traveller's shifting perspective and knowledge. But, as the interchangeability of metaphor suggests, this is not a simple progress from error to enlightenment, but a recurrent confusion, intrinsic to the act of perception. 'Critical eyes' develop their own species of error: scepticism can itself be an optical illusion. The poem's concern with topographical nicety stresses the capricious partiality of all points of view:

> But far down and near barn and I
> Since then have smiled,
> Having seen my new cautiousness
> By itself beguiled
>
> To disdain what seemed the barn
> Till a few steps changed
> It past all doubt to the down;
> So the barn was avenged.

Perception and valuation are closely intertwined, as the poem suggests; and error is integral to this process. The fallible eye has no privileged standpoint but is caught up in the body's shifting relations with a dense, bafflingly external world.

[102]

The mind's estrangement from nature is frequently posited, in the poems, in spatial terms which stress the contradiction between the self as infinite subject (whose horizons comprehend receding perspectives of time and space) and as finite object, situated at a merely contingent centre in a limited, vulnerable body. This is the theme of 'Health':

> Four miles at a leap, over the dark hollow land,
> To the frosted steep of the down and its junipers black,
> Travels my eye with equal ease and delight:
> And scarce could my body leap four yards.
>
> This is the best and worst of it –
> Never to know,
> But to imagine gloriously, pure health.

The mind's element is change, desire overleaps itself, and content is an abstraction from the conflicts of an identity which, the ghost of an epistemological joke suggests ('I should have changed my mind'), cannot be dissociated from its context:

> For had I health I could not ride or run or fly
> So far or so rapidly over the land
> As I desire: I should reach Wiltshire tired;
> I should have changed my mind before I could be in Wales.
> I could not love; I could not command love.
> Beauty would still be far off
> However many hills I climbed over;
> Peace would still be farther.
> Maybe I should not count it anything
> To leap these four miles with the eye;
> And either I should not be filled almost to bursting with
>   desire,
> Or with my power desire would still keep pace.

Despite the Whitmanesque measures and the reiterated 'I' there is an aspiring urgency to the syntax here quite different from the placid celebratory parataxis of Whitman's verse. 'Health' reveals the contradictions within which the self moves, in its encounters with a world at once obstructively other and yet entering into all the intimacy of consciousness. Mind rests at ease upon the horizon's rim, and yet simultaneously strives to transcend the pathetically circumscribed body within which it is confined.

It might seem that such encounters of a mind and a landscape are purely private experiences. Indeed, William James's Pragmatism has consistently been seen as the rationale of an extreme, relativistic individualism, and this is the direction taken by the literary adaptation of the 'stream of consciousness'. But James's phenomenology is anchored in a conviction of the social, cultural sources of individual experience. Its basic proposition, perhaps, is that the significance felt to inhere within the diversity of private experiences is an historic deposit, the silt of generations of human evolution. *The Briefer Course* (1892), for example, is emphatic about this, claiming, as the major discovery of modern science,

> the gradually growing conviction that *mental life is primarily teleological*; ... that our various ways of thinking and feeling have grown to be what they are because of their utility in shaping our *reactions* on the outer world, ... that the essence of mental life and bodily life are one, namely 'the adjustment of inner to outer relations'.

Thus, when he speaks of the 'physical environment', James is discussing an already socialized phenomenon. 'Nature' – more widely, 'the external world' – has, in the course of evolution, become a cultural category, definable only in its relation to the collectivity of individual consciousnesses for whom it is the ground, vehicle and object of their self-articulation. James's propositions find a more poetic notation in Thomas's words:

> The eye that sees the things of today, and the ear that
> hears, the mind that contemplates or dreams, is itself an
> instrument of an antiquity equal to whatever it is called
> upon to apprehend. (*SC*, p. 156)

This functional adjustment of consciousness and reality
means that all perception is an interpretative recreation
of a world unknowable in its essence, realized only
within particular and therefore selective views:

> And as for seeing things as in themselves they really are,
> ... what is a fine summer's day as in itself it really is?
> Is the meteorological office to decide? or the poet? or the
> farmer? (*DC*, 14 July 1903)

For Thomas 'meaning' is just irrefutably *there*, built
into the structure of the perceived world, as he suggests
in his discussion of Hardy's use of landscape:

> ... just as the plains of Enna are inseparable from
> Persephone's grief, or the hyacinths from the remorse
> of Apollo. All landscape is capable of this; indeed, all
> landscape has done the same; and there is not a tree, nor
> does any sunset pass, that is not charged with human
> aspiration and passion. (*DC*, 6 December 1901)

Yet for Thomas this 'charge' of meaning is problematic,
to be apprehended only through some mystical intuition
of 'oneness' with the soul of things, rather than a
transparent, open sense of human and natural continuity. When he speaks of the individual's relation to
the landscape, he almost invariably speaks in terms of
a mystery in which an intuitive conviction of consanguinity is undercut by a sense of actual disaffiliation.
This he spells out in an early review of Maeterlinck
which seems a remote foreshadowing of the poem 'It
rains':

> We would have him remember that so long as we possess

bodies that are palsied with the mysteries of aeons, grief and love, and hope and fear, and innumerable complex emotions, like the melancholy on a cold, solitary evening in early spring, will never be solved, except by a millenial race that has never experienced them. Perhaps we shall be permitted to smile at their solutions even then. (*DC*, 28 April 1902)

The mystery here is identified with a wonder-sickness that has primordial, biological roots; yet perhaps the most significant word is the transferred epithet 'solitary' – the sense of a pervasive, ontological solitude is allowed into consciousness through a gap opened up by a more immediate, social exclusion. The fact that 'value' has emerged from the historic encounter of mind and nature only intensifies the mystery of things. This, he suggests in the Introduction to Jefferies' *The Hills and the Vale*, where he alludes to James's *Varieties of Religious Experience*, is the significance of the mystical epiphany for Jefferies:

It is in the aspiration and the hope – in the sense of 'hovering on the verge of a great truth', of a 'meaning waiting in the grass and water', of a 'wider existence yet to be enjoyed on the earth' – in the 'increased consciousness of our own life', gained from sun and sky and sea . . . The mystic has a view of things by which all knowledge becomes real – or disappears – and all things are seen related to the whole in a manner which gives a wonderful value to the least of them, . . . a vague beauty imperfectly adumbrated, as was the meaning of the universe itself in his mood of 'thoughts without words mobile like the stream, nothing compact that can be grasped and stayed; dreams that slip silently as water slips through the fingers.' (pp. ix–xxxi)

Thomas's poetry abounds in attempts to seize hold of an inapprehensible core of meaning felt to lurk within the endlessly dissolving flux of things. This seizing of

[106]

the essence of a multitude of appearances can only be transient, intuitive and, it seems, intensely private. In 'The Unknown Bird' the desire to share an experience felt to be charged with significance meets with incredulity and rebuffs. The bird's solitary notes duplicate his own isolation. But its distance and unreality seem to reflect the unreality and distance of those others with whom he cannot share his perceptions. The only certainty seems to lie in the present moment of consciousness: 'This surely I know'. Memory blurs the experience, so that it cannot be definitively recalled. Yet at the same time, remoteness adds depth and resonance to the mystery. If he must define the bird's song – something 'bodiless sweet' contrasted with his own too solid flesh – he can do so only by speaking of its effects on him, in a succession of qualifications which turn back on and contradict each other, till we are left only with the sense of a vanishing experience. The continuity of this consciousness which extends backwards and forwards in time and spans innumerable complex moods is itself in doubt. The assertion of surety abounds with unspoken reservations – hinted at in that inability to 'make another hear', the sense of being 'in a dream'. It fears to be pinned down in a formula, prefers the infinite possibility of the imprecise and undefined ('if I must say', 'I cannot tell'), but in this very diffidence it too seems to evaporate. Is the 'I who listened then' the same I which now 'surely knows'? In thinking of the past, this I assumes a dreamlike volatility, moving beyond itself, through the conditional recall of the past into a future which cancels the present ('if I think of it, become . . .'). Is present or past self in some unexplained way responsible for the failure of communication, or does the failure lie with those others who could not be made to hear? The bird becomes, by the close of the poem, the projection of a *self* which, even when within reach, seems 'somehow distant still', perpetually elsewhere in the moment of trying to apprehend itself here and now. The self, that is, is a permanently deferred subject, and can never enter into the imaginary fullness of self-presence which it seeks. Like England, like Lob, it is realest at the very moment of disappearing.

Consciousness can perhaps find *its* unity and coherence by fusing all its data into some intuitive gestalt which leaves nothing over. But it is perpetually frustrated by an 'earth . . . absorbed in . . . growth and multiplication' (*SC*, p. 44) forever overflowing the mind which tries to hold it steady. The sense of insatiety and the fretful guilt which are noticeable features of both this poem and 'The Glory' arise from the incommensurability of overflowing world and comprehending mind. The opening phrase of 'The Glory' intends to distinguish intrinsic from pragmatic qualities, but succumbs to their immediate confusion, for 'glory' is not merely a subjective response and 'beauty' not even or simply an objective quality of matter. At the same time, perception's power to organize its data, as work ranges the new-mown hay, seems to be belied by the randomness with which details are accumulated. This contrast is underwritten by the dispersal to near invisibility of a rhyme scheme which haunts our reading with a ghostly hint of a subliminal order and coherence which, if we tried a little harder, we might just grasp. Such a tension issues in the exfoliating rhythm of search in the opening lines, where the delaying of the main verb 'invites' itself invites us on, enacting that expectancy which carries us through a sequence of uncompleted acts until we too are let fall with that empty-handed 'scorning':

> The glory of the beauty of the morning, –
> The cuckoo crying over the untouched dew;

The blackbird that has found it, and the dove
That tempts me on to something sweeter than love;
White clouds ranged even and fair as new-mown hay;
The heat, the stir, the sublime vacancy
Of sky and meadow and forest and my own heart: –
The glory invites me, yet it leaves me scorning
All I can ever do, all I can be,
Beside the lovely of motion, shape and hue,
The happiness I fancy fit to dwell
In beauty's presence. Shall I now this day
Begin to seek as far as heaven, as hell,
Wisdom or strength to match this beauty, start
And tread the pale dust pitted with small dark drops,
In hope to find whatever it is I seek,
Hearkening to short-lived, happy-seeming things
That we know naught of, in the hazel copse?
Or must I be content with discontent
As larks and swallows are perhaps with wings?
And shall I ask at the day's end once more
What beauty is, and what I can have meant
By happiness? And shall I let all go,
Glad, weary, or both? Or shall I perhaps know
That I was happy oft and oft before,
Awhile forgetting how I am fast pent,
How dreary-swift, with naught to travel to,
Is Time? I cannot bite the day to the core.

Verbs of unfolding action rise to a crescendo which is
never attained, as the syntax is deflected into momentary
pauses, 'in beauty's presence', 'in the hazel copse', before
being roused again to further enquiries: 'Begin to
seek . . . to match . . . start and tread . . . in hope to find
whatever it is I seek, hearkening . . . know naught of'.
The object can be defined only negatively, and the
sentence, in its climaxes and dispersals, reaches no
final goal, though in the progressive tautening of
the syntax up to the abrupt denouement, it seems to

approach a provisional resolution. The self-deprecation is the reflex of an external resistance. If he hesitates between seeking and letting go, the world also invites him and leaves him scorning. The disjunctions 'do/be/know' correspond to the differentiation of 'motion, shape and hue'. The alternative responses, and the division of mind from body ('wisdom or strength') reflect the diversity of the external world (heaven, hell; the high-flying lark, far-flying swallow; meadow, sky, forest). The coinage of new compounds ('happy-seeming', 'dreary-swift') suggests this ambivalence between pragmatic appearance and unknowable essence.

Thomas lapses repeatedly from suspecting a real essence awaiting capture to reluctant acquiescence in a purely pragmatic notion of value. This is apparent in 'The Glory' in the shift from the essential 'what beauty is' to the pragmatic 'what I can have meant/By happiness', and in that series of unanswered questions which only underlines the tenuousness of our knowledge about inner or outer worlds. The labyrinthine syntax unfolds a world in which appearances go spinning off in all directions. The initial feeling that concentrated effort of act or thought will somehow pierce the surface of things succumbs to the curiously double-edged conclusion. It may be better to lose oneself in the multitude of appearances, for the core may be bitter (hell, rather than heaven).

In 'The Glory' the quest turns into a flight, as if a mortified ego were fleeing its own inadequacy rather than seeking an emotion worthy of its object. The moment overflows because this 'sublime vacancy' is both that inherited fullness and harmony of earth and sky described in *The South Country*, the legacy of 'a thousand years of settled continuous government' and, conversely, a place of empty transit for the vagrant self, suspecting that there is no 'core' and that he is

[110]

betrayed into a mere 'respect for surfaces' while 'concerned twenty-four hours a day about the difficulty of living'. The poem fluctuates therefore between an existential ethic of personal satisfaction and a fitful intuition that there is some wider system of meanings with which the mind might engage but which remains 'a mystery'.

This tension lies behind that symbolism of a quest which is also a flight which abounds in Thomas's writings, and is spelt out in *The South Country* in a passage which throws light on innumerable poems:

> But it is hard to make anything like a truce between the two incompatible desires, the one for going on and on over the earth, the other that would settle for ever, in one place as in a grave and have nothing to do with change . . . The two desires will often painfully alternate. (p.186)

The search for a lost home and a postulated ideal self which is also a refusal of inadequacy lies at the heart of Thomas's mystery. It recurs throughout the work as an analogy for the structure of consciousness, caught at the intersection of fixity and flux. In 'The Other', this is allegorically embodied by splitting the self into an anxious emotionally volatile pursuer, racked not only by desire but by 'Desire of desire', and a pursued other who is an 'unseen moving goal'. For the self is at once a continuity transcending time and caught up in every moment in the eddying, amorphous current of experience.

Nowhere is this clearer than in 'The Signpost', which expresses the circling volatility of the self by dissociating it, on the one hand, into a series of self-cancelling voices and, on the other, into a series of external signs by which these alternative possible selves are articulated. The self, poised between external and internal, is constituted in the act of reading which mediates between voices and sign, a reading which is itself a site of mere empty passage, like the crossroads at which he pauses:

> I read the sign. Which way shall I go?
> A voice says: You would not have doubted so
> At twenty. Another voice gentle with scorn
> Says: At twenty you wished you had never been born.

Both voices are inflexions of the subject here and now, but so, one might add, are older and younger selves, and that younger self was equally divided between totally contrary moods. The gentle scorn, which initially appears to be directed at the younger self, is in fact a response to one inflexion of the self here and now, in a doubling of that reproach about present doubt which in some way dismisses it as patronizingly as it dismisses the self-dramatizing youthful self. This subject actually exists only in the momentary present, its past and future selves as unreal as the options it contemplates and the voices into which it disperses. But this dispersal in turn decentres the supposedly actual subject, rendering it too unreal, pushing it out of its place as the voices take over the discourse. A crossroads is nothing in itself, a mere empty intersection where roads meet, like that described in *The South Country*: 'A crossing of roads encloses a waste place of no man's land' (p. 11). By the same token, the self is that 'no man', simply a crossroads where its own imaginary voices meet. The idea of an original, self-constituting being evaporates in this whirling proliferation of voices, which rapidly come to ignore the poet himself, to engage in conversation among themselves, turning him into a mere eaves-dropper who at one point nervously joins in their laughter so as not to feel totally excluded.

This marginalizing of the subject is reinforced by the detailed attention to the external scene, which though it everywhere contains omens of change and loss, seems to go on without reference to him:

One hazel lost a leaf of gold
From a tuft at the tip, when the first voice told
The other he wished to know what 'twould be
To be sixty by this same post. 'You shall see'
He laughed – And I had to join in his laughter –
'You shall see; but either before or after,
Whatever happens, it must befall,
A mouthful of earth to remedy all
Regrets and wishes shall freely be given . . .'

What happens throughout the poem is a repeated displacement of the supposedly authoritative, decision-making, self-directing subject. The world seems initially no more than the changing and contingent context for this self to make its choices in. Yet increasingly he seems dependent on that world for his options. In that sense, the self is no more than an ensemble of voices, uttering mere empty speculative words that take no purchase on the real, but simply yearn towards a lost past and an unattainable future in regrets and wishes. Ironically, then, the remedy which cuts short this illusory self's fantasies of freedom is 'freely given', doesn't have to be struggled for but comes out of the blue, and blocks the site of that supposed freedom with a gross physical obstruction, 'a mouthful of earth'.

This death is something which is prefigured in all the unconstrued signs with which the poem opened, the dim sea glinting chill, the shy white sun, the 'skeleton weeds', grasses white with frost, and the 'smoke' of the traveller's joy with its omen of vagrancy and transience. The poem then closes with the peroration of the second voice, mocking at a subject which defines itself simply in terms of the hollow 'freedom to wish', and slyly suggesting that, when all these questions have been answered and remedied, that posthumous future self might find that all antitheses and choices are less important than the opportunity to choose:

> '. . . and your wish may be
> To be here or anywhere talking to me,
> No matter what the weather, on earth,
> At any age between death and birth,
> To see what day or night can be,
> The sun and the frost, the land and the sea,
> Summer, Autumn, Winter, Spring,
> With a poor man of any sort, down to a king'

Just as the subject had initially been marginalized by place, so now place ('here or anywhere') is in turn devalued. There is no change of place, for he will still be standing by the same signpost at sixty, yearning then, perhaps, back to this now past-present. The subject is no more than this moment of poised wishfulness, always on the point of choosing a route, never actually doing so. At the end of the poem, he still stands on the threshold of that choice which preoccupies him here and now, in a further complicating displacement of willing and wishing which leaves him a vacant nexus of desires and unanswered questions, '"Wondering where he shall journey, O where?"'

Repeatedly in his poems we find Thomas poised at some threshold of transit and pause, at a crossroads here and in 'Aspens', entering town in 'Good-night', crossing an horizon ridge and stile in 'Over the Hills', stepping over the doorstep in 'The New House'. In 'The Bridge' he has 'come a long way today' and stands now, paused, 'On a strange bridge alone'. The bridge is a figure of life itself, where the moment of lived experience is always with us and yet perpetually slipping away. He will always be here, with the past 'no more / Tonight than a dream', the 'dark-lit stream' drowning future and past. The bridge is a place of paradox, for it is a place of passage and of rest at once, a moment of calling up

[114]

and hiding simultaneously. If at the beginning he remembers old friends, at the end 'the Night's first lights / And shades hide what has never been, / Things goodlier, lovelier, dearer than will be or have been'. With past and future alike under erasure, the bridge becomes almost a place of security, for here 'No traveller has rest more blest / Than this moment brief between two lives'. The bridge is 'strange' because he stands on it as a perpetual stranger, forever estranged from past and future lives, past and future worlds. The power of the symbolism derives from the way it concretely embodies an impossible destiny, the self forced to abandon its past, a no longer tenable order founded on 'a thousand years of settled continuous government', and yet never arriving at some unspecifiable new destination. In the end it is the lost possibilities of 'what has never been' which seize the imagination, and these are, of course, 'goodlier, lovelier, dearer, than will be or have been'. What we see in these accumulated comparatives is, in fact, a crisis of value in Thomas's poetry, a repeated interrogation of inner and outer worlds which have been called into question by this paralysis at the very moment of transition, this sense of being forever transfixed in the 'moment brief' of enjambment 'between / Two lives'.

That line in 'The Signpost', 'With a poor man of any sort down to a king', indicates the origin of this crisis of value. For the hierarchies of privilege which place the man in the manor house or a king at the top of the scale can no longer be justified. Invert the scale, take poverty as the natural condition of an earthbound species (whose only 'freely given' portion, after all, is 'a mouthful of earth'), take riches as a burden, and the king becomes the lowest and most dejected wretch of fortune. 'The Owl' is a poem which explores the careful comparatives of privilege.

[115]

Here the wandering self seeks momentary shelter from the elements in a place of rest which can never be a home. In privation, he grasps the relativity of all values, pragmatically defined in relation to immediate needs and pressures, shifting from moment to moment as they change. By its close, the poem has moved out to embrace that larger, social spectrum within which values are articulated and assessed.

The privations of the first stanza can be borne, because they seem at the midpoint on some relative scale between absolute exhaustion and rest which, in a reduced scheme of expectations, seems 'the sweetest thing under a roof'. When shelter is gained, however, the limits of tolerance shift. The world he has left outside now seems implacably hostile, while the once valued creature comforts dwindle to commonplace. As, previously, the present had been sustained by the hope of improvement, now it is underwritten by the memory of what it has left behind. The shift of comparative values has been an entirely private one: as its environment changes, the self reassesses, on a purely internal scale, the criteria of tolerance. But the owl's cry awakens another realization: that beyond this island of comfort lies a vaster world of scarcity and want, which turns the poet's own minimal pleasures into a cameo of luxury and self-indulgence. The guilt which elsewhere seems an excessive, morbid rehearsal of personal inadequacy before the majesty of nature here takes on a specifically social cast, as he acknowledges those others on whose destitution he is in some unspecified way an unwilling parasite, 'all who lay under the stars, / Soldiers and poor, unable to rejoice'.

The cultural origins of this crisis of value are revealed in the poem 'Tears', where a temporary coming together, and a dissolution, illumine both inner and outer worlds with value. The poem also suggests the source of the insecurity at the heart of experience, accounting for the emotional bankruptcy acknowledged in the terse opening sentence:

> It seems I have no tears left. They should have fallen –
> Their ghosts, if tears have ghosts, did fall – that day
> When twenty hounds streamed by me, not yet combed out
> But still all equals in their rage of gladness
> Upon the scent, made one, like a great dragon
> In Blooming Meadow that bends towards the sun
> And once bore hops: and on that other day
> When I stepped out from the double-shadowed Tower
> Into an April morning, stirring and sweet
> And warm. Strange solitude was there and silence.
> A mightier charm than any in the Tower
> Possessed the courtyard. They were changing guard,
> Soldiers in line, young English countrymen,
> Fair-haired and ruddy, in white tunics. Drums
> And fifes were playing 'The British Grenadiers'.
> The men, the music piercing that solitude
> And silence, told me truths I had not dreamed,
> And have forgotten since their beauty passed.

At first this sounds like a conventional patriotic piece, out of Housman and Sir John Squire. Yet what is striking is the inability of the traditional rituals to hold the mind's allegiance for more than an instant. Their 'truth', as witnesses to an abiding Englishness, has to be invented afresh in each instance by the superficial beauty of the spectacle. Past and future, which faith in cultural continuity should hold in easy alliance, in fact dissolve into private nullity, lost as soon as found. This, surely, accounts for the *strangeness* of the solitude, for the threatening ambivalence of the 'double-shadowed Tower', for the otherwise gratuituous hint of change in the meadow that 'once bore hops', as well as for the contained menace of the dragon, rival of St George and therefore of England. The poet is excluded from the

[117]

sense of corporate identity in which hounds and soldiers alike are 'made one'. But perhaps this is itself an illusory unity: the dogs are only momentarily 'all equals'.

The self, finding only the ghost of an emotional response, knows deep down that the undreamed 'truths' can be sustained only momentarily by a superficial, transitory 'beauty'. His own forgetting then sunders once more surface and essence. What persists is an estranging solitude and silence, the self cut off both from language and solidarity. The gulf opened up between 'English countrymen' and 'British Grenadiers' is like that we have seen in 'The Combe'. The former are innocent in their pastoral pathos; the latter carries the burden of an imperial ideology and the exultant violence which sustains it. The two concepts define that gap in Englishness where allegiance founders, as the poet realized in the comments recalled by Edward Garnett in his introduction to the *Selected Poems* in 1927: 'I don't think I could alter "Tears" to make it marketable. I feel that the correction you want made is only essential if the whole point is in the British Grenadiers as might be expected in these times.' The 'charm', it may be, is that of a hypnotic ideological magic, seducing both young men and poet to an unnecessary and pointless death. Allegiance to such images may be misplaced. Hence, perhaps, the guilty self-reproach in the opening lines, and the refusal to spell out these ineffable truths. If he is emotionally bankrupt, unable any more to respond spontaneously to the traditional symbols, the fault, though he refuses to admit it, may lie with those symbols, not with the self.

It is in the *symbol* that the enigma of value is focused for Thomas. In his study of the Belgian Symbolist, *Maurice Maeterlinck* (1911), he cites *The Varieties of Religious Experience* to explain a distinction between counters and symbols:

'Most of us,' says James, 'can remember the strangely moving power of passages in certain poems we read when we were young; irrational doorways . . . through which the mystery of fact, the wildness and the pang of life stole into our hearts . . . The words have now perhaps become mere polished surfaces for us; but lyric poetry and music are alive and significant only in proportion as they fetch these vague vistas of a life continuous with our own, beckoning and inviting, yet ever eluding our pursuit. We are alive or dead to the eternal inner message of the arts according as we have kept or lost this mystical susceptibility.' (pp. 30–2)

The passage explains the inviting and elusive beauty of 'The Glory' and the mystery of 'The Unknown Bird'; it suggests the significance of the music in 'The Gypsy', 'Tears', 'The Penny Whistle' and other poems; and it explains, too, the symbolism of the threshold in Thomas's work. Its most direct echo, however, is 'The Path', a poem which, while it is a faithful transcription of an ordinary English scene, simultaneously talks about itself, employs the path as a symbol of its own progress from start to finish. For, like the path itself, the poem opens up, in James's words, 'vague vistas of a life continuous with our own, beckoning and inviting', yet returns us at its end to 'the mystery of fact' itself. The path, we are told, 'serves / Children for looking down . . . to where / A fallen tree checks the sight'. Men and women are not interested in what its irrational doorway offers, contented with the road 'and what the children tell'. The aureate language with which the poet describes the path ('like silver', 'gold, olive, and emerald', 'silvered') suggests that he has travelled it and shares the children's values. They 'wear' the path, but they have not 'polished' it into insignificance; rather they have 'silvered' it 'With the current of their feet', endowing it with more, not less, value. Nevertheless, there is a hint of dispossession here too, for

[119]

                                             the eye
    Has but the road, the wood that overhangs
    And underyawns it, and the path that looks
    As if it led to some legendary
    Or fancied place where men have wished to go
    And stay; till, sudden, it ends where the wood ends.

And where the poem ends too. Poem and path alike
depart from the main road, but they lead to no 'legendary
or fancied place', simply back to the ordinary mystery
from which they started. The poem's 'legendary' dimension lies in the rite of passage itself (the children also
live in narrative, 'tell' of what they see there). It is
because sight is checked that fancy can flourish; as so
often in Thomas's verse, the very fact of being hidden
endows something with significance. Once again, however, part of the magic depends upon the emptiness of
the landscape, for 'the road is houseless, and leads not
to school'. It is in their very abandonment that poetry
and place alike awaken our 'mystical susceptibility'.
   Such a mood is never far away when Thomas contemplates the mysterious power of the symbol to grip
our imagination. In the 'Dedication' to *The Icknield
Way*, for example, the road itself becomes a symbol:

> I know there is nothing beyond the farthest of far ridges
> except a signpost to unknown places. The end is in the
> means – in the sight of that beautiful long straight line of
> the Downs in which a curve is latent – in the houses we
> shall never enter, with their dark secret windows and
> quiet hearth-smoke, or their ruins friendly only to elders
> and nettles – in the people passing whom we shall never
> know though we may love them . . . This book . . . is,
> however, in some ways a fitting book for me to write. For it
> is about a road which begins many miles before I could
> come on its traces and ends miles beyond where I had to
> stop . . . I could not find a beginning or an end of the

Icknield Way. It is thus a symbol of mortal things with their beginnings and ends always in immortal darkness. (p. vi)

It is beginnings and endings which endow the road with mystery, yet the mystery is inherent in the road itself, just as the end is in the means, and that mystery is most apparent as a *social* event, in the 'dark secret windows' of 'houses we shall never enter' which immediately give way to an image of deeper dispossession, 'ruins friendly only to elders and nettles'. The 'people passing' then take on a profounder symbolic value. It is significant that they are going *in the opposite direction*; it is as if the poet were almost perversely bound away in pursuit of 'nothing' more significant than 'a signpost to unknown places'. But the 'unknown' is present here and now, in those 'whom we shall never know though we may love them'. In this discrepancy between knowledge and love lies the key to Thomas's theory of symbolism.

The distinction between symbols and counters, which Thomas considers at length in his book on Pater, also crops up in *The South Country*, when he reflects on how nature has the power suddenly to thrust before our eyes images of Eden which derive their power from the fact that they seem already archaic, 'as if she silently recorded the backward dreams of each generation and reproduced them for us unexpectedly'. After recounting one such scene, a chance observed encounter of drover boy and gypsies on a July early morning, he remarks: 'These things also propose to the roving, unhistoric mind an Eden, one still with us, one that is passing, not, let us hope, the very last.' Such scenes –

come to have a rich symbolical significance; they return persistently, and, as it were, ceremoniously – on festal days – but meaning I know not what . . . Something in me belongs to these things, but I hardly think that the mere naming of them will mean anything except to those . . .

who have experienced the same. A great writer so uses the words of everyday that they become a code of his own which the world is bound to learn and in the end take unto itself. But words are no longer symbols, and to say 'hill' or 'beech' is not to call up images of a hill or a beech-tree, since we have so long been in the habit of using the words for beautiful and mighty and noble things very much as a book-keeper uses figures without seeing gold and power. I can, therefore, only try to suggest what I mean by the significance of the plant in the stoneheap, the wet lilac, the misty cliff, by comparing it with that of scenes in books where we recognize some power beyond the particular and personal. (pp. 135–6)

Thomas's most famous poem, 'Old Man', has one of its sources in this passage. The poem is also concerned with the gap between love and knowledge, between having 'a rich symbolical significance' and 'meaning I know not what', between naming and experiencing, words and suggestion. At the centre of the poem, as of the above passage, is the sense of an expulsion from Eden. Once, it was possible to apprehend language and reality in their mysterious intersection; experience was unified. Now, however, things fall apart. Language no longer inheres in the thing it describes, as the very contradictoriness of the herb's names suggests: 'in the name there's nothing / To one that knows not Lad's-love, or Old Man'. Such names are both superficial and obfuscating, 'Half decorate, half perplex, the thing it is'. What that is, in turn, 'clings not to the names / In spite of time'. But if the external world is divided – between the *Ding an sich* and its various signifiers – so too is the internal world of the subject.

The poet may be 'one that knows it well', but the perplexity which inheres in the bush also invades his mind. He likes the names but not the herb, but only because 'for certain / I love it', and this distinction between liking and loving opens up a further gap, between himself and the child who, he believes, will also some day love it. That the child will only love it in the future suggests that love is something that grows with mystery. For her, now, the herb is not yet a locus of mystery, but a pure and immediate sensuous event, without past or future – that Edenic unity of experience from which he has been expelled, hence the echo of the primal paternal forbidding in an earlier garden which closes the paragraph:

> Often she waits there, snipping the tips and shrivelling
> The shreds at last on to the path, perhaps
> Thinking, perhaps of nothing, till she sniffs
> Her fingers and runs off. The bush is still
> But half as tall as she, though it is as old;
> So well she clips it. Not a word she says;
> And I can only wonder how much hereafter
> She will remember, with that bitter scent,
> Of garden rows, and ancient damson-trees
> Topping a hedge, a bent path to a door,
> A low thick bush beside the door, and me
> Forbidding her to pick.

Though he knows more than her, it is precisely his knowledge which makes him less than her and less than the omniscient God of *Genesis*. In his wondering about how much she will remember, the enjambment pause on that 'me' which ends the list reveals an anxiety that he may one day be expelled once more from Eden, cast out of her memories of the scene.

The child's 'nothing' is paradoxically full, a fullness of self-presence in which she needs nothing else. His 'nothing' on the contrary is sheer lack, a hungry, wondering void. To say 'in the name there's nothing' is to speak only of deprivation, of meaning withheld. What he fears for her is what he has already experi-

[123]

enced, a loss in which nevertheless meaning, like love, is generated by the very withholding of meaning, of which the herb's scent becomes the impalpable figure:

> As for myself,
> Where first I met the bitter scent is lost.
> I, too, often shrivel the grey shreds,
> Sniff them and think and sniff again and try
> Once more to think what it is I am remembering,
> Always in vain. I cannot like the scent,
> Yet I would rather give up others more sweet,
> With no meaning, than this bitter one.

Anxiety, of a muted kind, pervades the poem, enacted in the very rhythm of that sentence which in its repeated sniffings and thinkings touches no goal. In the final paragraph, this 'nothing' grows until it threatens to engulf the self, invading each sense in turn, expelling him once again from the garden out into that 'nothing beyond the farthest of far ridges' he had spoken of in *The Icknield Way*. The scent, that is, becomes 'a signpost to unknown places' outside mind and language altogether. By the time we enter the nameless avenue of the final line, that 'nothing' in the name of the opening line has turned into a menacing and positive power, like the 'accumulated gloom' that haunted a garden in *Oxford*, which raised 'the whole question between silence and speech, and did not answer it':

Underneath the shrubs the gloom is a presence . . . You watch and watch – like children who have found the lion's cage, but the lion invisible – until, gradually . . . you see that the caged thing is – nothingness, in all its shadowy pomp and immeasurable power. Seated there, you could swear that the darkness was moving about, treading the boundaries. When first I saw it it was as new and strange as if I had seen the world before the sun, and withdrawing my eyes and looking at the fresh limes was like beholding the light of the first dawn arriving at Eden. (pp. 214–5)

In such a place, as he had said earlier, 'the loneliness of the place becomes intense, as if one were hidden far back in time, and one's self an anachronism' (p. 210). What haunts the subject in 'Old Man' is a sense of its vulnerability and transience. The herb's smell opens a doorway onto a dark avenue which, like the Icknield Way, is 'a symbol of mortal things, with their beginnings and ends always in immortal darkness.' Yet, as so often in the poems, it is an exclusion from language and from solidarity which adds the deepest pang. The only speech in the poem is that act of forbidding at its centre. At the end, it is the absence of all those affiliations and affinities, so powerfully present in their accumulated negatives, which leaves the self exposed to immortal darkness:

> I have mislaid the key. I sniff the spray
> And think of nothing; I see and I hear nothing;
> Yet seem, too, to be listening, lying in wait
> For what I should, yet never can, remember:
> No garden appears, no path, no hoar-green bush
> Of Lad's love, or Old Man, no child beside,
> Neither father nor mother, nor any playmate;
> Only an avenue, dark, nameless, without end.

It would be easy to leave this poem insulated in its personal distress, but its sources in the prose release its historical secret, a secret not eluded by calling up metaphysical paradigms from *Genesis*. I have suggested already that a passage in *The South Country* is one major source, but I did not quote the context in full, since it is at least a whole chapter (that called 'June'), in which Jefferies and Thomas Traherne are invoked, as well as Malory, in speaking of 'men and women [who] survive only in the turns which their passionate hearts gave to these ghostly, everlastingly wandering tales'. One element in the chapter, however, provides the closest contact with these reflections, just preceding that quoted above. Thomas had spoken of looking back to a golden age of childhood in which 'The vastness and splendour and gloom of a world not understood, but seen in its effects and hardly at all in its processes, made a theatre which . . . glorify it exceedingly', and cited one instance, seen from a train, of a man and child walking beside a pond and 'the child stooping for a flower and its gossip unheard'. He goes on:

> Perhaps the happiest childhoods are those which pass completely away and leave whole tracts of years without a memory . . . I watch the past as I have seen workless, homeless men leaning over a bridge to watch the labours of a titanic crane and strange workers below in the ship running to and fro and feeding the crane. I recall green fields, one or two whom I loved in them, and though no trace of such happiness as I had remains, the incorruptible tranquillity of it all breeds fancies of great happiness. I recall many scenes . . . ladslove and tall, crimson, bitter dahlias in a garden – the sweetness of large, moist yellow apples eaten out of doors . . . [O]nly an inmost true self that desires and is in harmony with joy can perform these long journeys . . . (p. 133)

'Strange' here takes on a precise, historical significance, suggesting not a metaphysical estrangement but a social and economic movement in which cheaper casual labour was imported to undercut the domestic labour market, one of the issues focused by the dockers' strike of 1889, of which one leader was the 'glorious, great and good' John Burns. Only eight years before this was written, a strike by the London waterfront workers had been broken with the help of blackleg labour carried up the Thames by ship; in 1911 the same tactic was repeated; in 1912 the London and in 1913 the Dublin dockers' strikes were broken (David Kynaston, *King Labour*, 1976, pp. 140–2, 163–4).

The poem, written in December 1914, suppresses the historical resonances of the prose, which links the condition of the 'workless, homeless men' with that of a vagrant 'inmost true self'; but this is exactly how the symbol derives its suggestive power. 'Leaving Town' the opening chapter of *The Heart of England*, begins and ends with the Watercress Man, a 'traveller . . . a strange, free man', who seems a figure of Lob, an 'old man' envied by the boy, clearly a projection of the young Thomas, who observes him. But the suburban desert the poet is summoned to leave here itself shares in this 'strangeness'. It is the strangeness of a historical crisis of significance, in which meaning in its fullness at once overflows and evaporates:

> [T]hese streets are the strangest thing in the world. They have never been discovered. They cannot be classified. There is no tradition about them . . . They are . . . so new that we have inherited no certain attitude towards them, of liking or dislike . . . They suggest so much that they mean nothing at all. The eye strains at them as at Russian characters which are known to stand for something beautiful or terrible; but there is no translator: it sees a thousand things which at the moment of seeing are significant, but they obliterate one another. (ch. i)

The passage goes on to that description of a 'ruined Eden' quoted in an earlier chapter. The whole sequence echoes with the epithet 'strange', and it is not until he comes upon 'a sign-post that stood boldly up with undoubted inscriptions, one of them to London, and away from that I set my face' that, in flight, he seems to find some meaning. 'In the name there's nothing': 'They suggest so much that they mean nothing at all'. The paradoxical fullness of meaning which turns into emptiness is precisely what both names and scent of the herb 'old man' signify for the poet. But whereas in the prose this withholding of meaning is part of the curse of a ruined Eden, in the poetry it is the very guarantee of its richness and authenticity. Nevertheless, in both cases it is the sense of loss and exclusion which prevails, as 'Old Man' ends in that frightening dissolution of certainties in the 'avenue, dark, nameless, without end'. In this antithesis – the inverse ratio – of suggestion and meaning, only the symbol 'That hinted all and nothing spoke' can momentarily integrate the fractured experience of a subject who is a stranger to himself. The symbols speak, as in 'I never saw that land before',

> A language not to be betrayed;
> And what was hid should still be hid
> Excepting from those like me made
> Who answer when such whispers bid.

It is the very secretiveness of such meanings that guarantees their power. These symbols are not counters, they cannot be translated and pinned down into the kind of positive utterance that appealed to Thomas's father, or the jingo phrases that excite fat patriots, bards and journalists. Yet in their ineffability they endear, tell us that all is well, though they speak of a land 'I never saw . . . before, / And now can never see . . . again'.

Contemporary symbolist poetry represented for Thomas a crisis in the negotiation of public and private meanings. Symbols are social artefacts, the common currency of a shared culture. When they become esoteric, this reflects a rupture in the seamless web of meanings that culture takes for granted. Discussing symbolism in *Maurice Maeterlinck*, Thomas remarks: 'It may be that a day will come when the force of Mr Yeats's genius will have added to common culture the special knowledge through which alone the poem is intelligible. At present, the language is . . . dead or merely private' (pp. 30–2). He noted elsewhere of Yeats: 'At his best his poetry is fine because its symbols are natural, ancient, instinctive, not invented' (*MP*, 17 December 1908). One of the central concerns of *Maeterlinck* is the distinction between traditional and modern ideas of the symbol. Maeterlinck's own symbolism is implacably private, 'nothing but a series of fantastic images in a feverish man's brain'. Symbolism should not be problematic but, as he noted in a review, a grasping of the inevitable, for 'most poetry is carelessly pregnant in symbols, as Nature is' (*MP*, 13 April 1908). What lies behind the privatization of symbolism in poetry is a crisis of a wider kind, in which 'nature' itself is stripped of symbolic value.

'It is an old opinion that all visible things are symbols', he says in *Maeterlinck*. In the past it was assumed that reality was symbolic because it expressed some divine meaning immanent in nature: 'Sallustius . . . held the world itself to be a great myth, and the myths to be all allegories . . . For him the value of a thing lay "not in itself, but in the spiritual meaning which it hides and reveals."' Such hiding and revealing is, of course, typical of Thomas, but he found a rationale for it that did not need supernatural sanction in that chapter of James's *Talks to Students* which he cites. There James writes of some settlements in North Carolina which, in their 'rudimentariness and denudation', he found oppressively 'hideous' and 'ugly'.

The reaction of the inhabitants is quite different – pride in getting the wilderness 'under cultivation', revealing suddenly to James 'the whole inward significance of the situation', for to them James's 'mere ugly picture on the retina' was 'a symbol redolent with moral memories and sang a very paean of duty, struggle and success' (pp. 231–4). Thomas has a similar equivocal response to the industrialization of a Welsh village in

'Mothers and Sons' (*Rest and Unrest* pp. 49–92). At first, a tourist aesthete, he is found with one of those sons 'complaining together in raptures of regret about the growth of the village', and the ensuing despoliation. The mother of the title, however, sees it as bringing 'jobs for men', and the essay, one of Thomas's finest, concludes with a 'paean' to what the old woman represents:

> She welcomed the new without forgetting the old and gave both their due because she felt – she would never have said it, for she would have considered such high thinking arrogant – that the new and the old, the institutions, the reforms, the shops, the drainage system, were the froth made by the deep tide of men's inexpressible perverse desires.

It is the plight of the traveller that, as in 'Good-night', he should recognize this symbolic power and yet be unable to penetrate its mystery, experiencing it simply therefore as 'magic'. James speaks of a landscape which tells a story. Thomas's consummate little lyric, 'A Tale', has been described as an 'Imagist' poem in its directness and brevity. But as its title indicates, it absolutely denies the 'Imagist' aim of presenting a 'clean' image, of an object stripped of human accretions. Though nothing happens in the poem, it *is* a tale, replete with history, offering everywhere fragments of an everlasting testament. The story is there, still, for the sympathetic eye to read off, though it only deepens the melancholy with a reminder of what has been lost:

> There once the walls
> Of the ruined cottage stood.
> The periwinkle crawls
> With flowers in its hair into the wood.
>
> In flowerless hours
> Never will the bank fail,

With everlasting flowers
On fragments of blue plates, to tell the tale.

Thomas wrote in *The South Country* of this unobtrusive tale-telling:

> In some places history has wrought like an earthquake, in others like an ant or mole; everywhere, permanently; so that if we but knew or cared, every swelling of the grass, every wavering line of hedge or path or road were an inscription, brief as an epitaph, in many languages and characters. But most of us know only a few of these unspoken languages of the past, and only a few words in each. Wars and parliaments are but dim, soundless, and formless happenings in the brain; toil and passion of generations produce only an enriching of the light within the glades, and a solemnizing of the shadows. (p. 155)

The word 'epitaph' is, perhaps, the significant one. For James, initiation into knowledge brings significance; but for Thomas it is in the continuing gap between knowledge and love that the mysterious meaningfulness of these chance, momentary encounters is bred. The subject will never master all these lost tongues: he has 'mislaid the key'. And indeed throughout Thomas's prose it is this indecipherability which adds peculiar poignancy to his vision. *The Heart of England* almost seems, at times, a disquisition on symbolism which speaks with the obliquity it describes. It abounds in narratives where the journey becomes the symbol of some larger transit in which meaning is lost and never quite recovered, and yet the intuition of its presence offers a melancholy joy more intense than actually grasping it. The linguistic metaphor recurs. Of poppies in a field, for example, he writes, 'Something in me desired them, might even seem to have long ago possessed and lost them, but when thought followed vision . . .

[131]

I could not understand their importance ... A book in a foreign, unknown language which is known to be full of excellent things is a simple possession and untantalizing compared with these' (p. 72). Elsewhere 'a dolmen rises out of the wheat in one field, like a quotation from an unknown language in the fair page of a book' (p. 114). Again, a farm waggon whose 'birth out of the shadow was a mighty thing that shared the idiom of stately trees and the motions of great waters' nevertheless 'suggested nothing definite, at least no history'; 'Dimly, uncertainly, profoundly, never quite expressing itself in any known language', lacking 'articulate power', it 'neither carried its legend on its exterior nor encouraged anything but a joyful surmise' (pp. 141–2).

'Sad more than joyful', but 'sad only with joy too, too far off / For me to taste it', Thomas's landscapes embody a double exile for the peripatetic self. On the one hand, he is cut off from the meanings of the suburban world which bred him. On the other, he is forever seeking reconciliation and reunion with the ruined Edens of a lost England which he believes are his true home. He is thus in actuality always on the road, his beginnings and ends in immortal darkness, caught in a perpetual vagrancy, a 'betweenness' in which bridge and stile and horizon ridge, the transient margins of dawn and twilight, become more universal symbols of that inter-face zone which is the true, historical site of being for the suburban, superfluous man, belonging to no class or race, having no traditions, muddy, confused, hesitat-ing, and yet 'world-conscious, and hence suffer[ing] unutterable loneliness'. In 'Words', he had spoken of English words as combining this strangeness and familiarity:

Strange as the races
Of dead and unborn:

Strange and sweet
Equally,
And famliar,
To the eye,
As the dearest faces
That a man knows
And as lost homes are . . .

Expelled from the lost homes of past and future, the world-conscious individual finds a home for his loneliness in the fixity and freedom of language, the family of words.

In *Talks to Students* James had said of the kind of epiphanies discussed in this chapter that 'This higher vision of an inner significance in what, until then, we had realized only in the dead external way, often comes over a person suddenly; and, when it does so, it makes an epoch in his history' (p. 242). In *The Heart of England*, a ballad singer in the parlour of a Welsh mountain inn leads Thomas to reflect on the power of the symbol in a way which shows its relation to his own 'lost homes':

> At some time, perhaps many times in his life, every man is likely to meet with a thing in art or nature or human life or books which astonishes him and gives him a profound satisfaction, not so much because it is rich or beautiful or strange, as because it is a symbol of a thing which, without the symbols, he could never grasp and enjoy . . . the world is one flame of these blossoms, could we but see. (p. 196)

The gap between sign and significance is where the subject finds, and loses, himself. Music, like poetry, is the expression of this tension between love and knowledge, in which the subject keeps faith with that which he cannot know but persists in believing possible:

Music, the rebel, the martyr, the victor – music, the romantic cry of matter striving to become spirit – is itself such a symbol, and there is no melody so poor that it will not at some time or other, to our watchful or receptive minds, have its festal hour ... (p. 197)

For significance to survive in a centrifugal age requires increasing vigilance on the part of the 'watchful or receptive minds' that wait upon the symbol. 'The old ballads and folk songs', Thomas says, in a passage which explains why such songs recur as theme and refrain in his own poems, are 'richest in the plain, immortal symbols', because –

The best of them seem to be written in a language that should be universal, if only simplicity were truly simple to mankind ... They are themselves epitomes of whole generations, of a whole countryside. They are the quintessence of many lives and passions made into a sweet cup for posterity. (pp. 197–8)

But, though the songs are vessels for a communion of past and present, they also deliver 'an oracle of solemn and ambiguous things'. It is, in reality, a brief and unreal communion, for in the end significance has to be supplied by the recipients, 'out of our own hearts', and part of that meaning is the very mystery by which the songs 'lend themselves to infinite interpretations', according to the listener's heart, and thereby 'move us suddenly and launch us into the unknown'.

The eternal note of nostalgia is unmistakable. A gulf opens, not only between past and present, but within the present itself, between the diverse private destinies and interpretations, momentarily linked in the universal language of song. Like the landscape, such songs remind us of what we have lost, and this loss is not only outside but within the self:

[134]

They are not art, they come to us imploring a new lease
of life on the sweet earth, and so we come to give them
something which the dull eye sees not in the words and
notes themselves, out of our own hearts, as we do when
we find a black hearthstone among the nettles . . .

The strangeness and looseness of its framework allowed
each man to see himself therein . . . or something possible
to a self which he desired to be or imagined himself to be,
or perhaps believed himself once to have been . . . And
that little inn, in the midst of mountains and immense
night, seemed a temple of all souls, where a few faithful
ones still burnt candles and remembered the dead. (*HE*,
ch. xl)

The gulf, in the end, is between what we are, superfluous men, and that forever ungraspable 'Other' which
is our true vocation. The episode itself is a potent
symbol. From the 'dim passage' of the inn a superfluous
man, in pursuit of his ideal self, stares 'through the
bar into the cloudy parlour' where men of his own
'race' who are strangers to him sing songs 'known to
them so well that they seemed not to listen'. Homeless,
he is not lost, for 'it is All Friends' Night, a traveller's
goodnight'. In a sense, he is one of the ghosts called
up by the song, 'That in the echo lives and with the echo
dies'.

James, in *Talks to Students*, speaks of his own 'flash
of insight' when 'looking at life with the eyes of a
remote spectator' he suddenly grasped that 'human life
in its wild intensity' was not 'dead and embalmed' but
'was there before me in the daily lives of the labouring
classes'. One instance of this produced a –

feeling of awe and reverence in looking at the peasant
women . . . Old hags . . . dried and brown and wrinkled . . .
envying nothing, humble-hearted, remote; – and yet . . .
bearing the whole fabric of the splendors and corruptions
of that city on their laborious back. For where would any

[135]

of it have been without their unremitting, unrewarding labour in the fields? (pp. 273–6).

'Mothers and Sons' expresses the same 'social mysticism' (Thomas's own phrase, of Traherne in *The South Country*). But so, too, does 'The Inn', where the superfluous man feels chastened in the face of such unassuming patience, yet shares too, momentarily, in a community of meanings that shows him where his true allegiance lies:

> 'Dolly Gray' I have heard sung all day by poor sluttish women as they gathered peas in the broad, burning fields of July, until it seemed that its terrible, acquiescent melody must have found a way to the stars and troubled them.

The symbol, for Thomas, becomes in the end a momentary place of community and exile together, for those modern men who belong nowhere. It is finally a *social* dilemma which endows such epiphanies with portentous power. The gulf between poet and peasant is vast; yet they share the same language and songs. The recurrent association of these moments with imagery of desolation, the hearthstone among the nettles, fragments of blue plate in a wood, a deserted chalk pit, suggest a desperate attempt to hold on to a dissolving cultural configuration. 'Nostalgia' is the private reflex of a tangible, historic and public moment. The conclusion of 'The Chalk Pit' hints at the teleology of that 'ontological wonder-sickness' (the phrase is James's) which haunts Thomas's writings. The poem is a dialogue between antithetical states of mind, a 'symbolist', who wants to fabricate fanciful scenarios from the empty chalk pit, peopling it with ghosts, and a 'pragmatist', who insists on its human significance, as 'a silent place that once rang loud' with human labour. The mystery at the heart of this emptiness is, in fact, an economic one. Men and

[136]

women once worked here. Their traces are everywhere.
It is the 'mystery of fact' which the place preserves, and
such traces make sense of and transfigure those otherwise terrifying 'nothings' which invest it, reducing
them to human proportions:

> 'You please yourself. I should prefer the truth
> Or nothing. Here in fact is nothing at all
> Except a silent place that once rang loud,
> And trees and us – imperfect friends, we men
> And trees since time began; and nevertheless
> Between us still we breed a mystery.'

IV

A Sense of Common Things

Thomas saw Maurice Maeterlinck's symbolist drama as a theatre of colliding solipsisms, a proliferation of monologues that never attained authentic speech, expressing the paradox in which we experience ourselves simultaneously as abstracted subjects, with a godlike superciliousness, and as impotent and pathetic objects, with an insect's futility:

> Life in this drama is a dream of a dream of a dream, refined, reduced, grey and remote, and very quiet. This is how we have come to see ourselves. Like gods we look down from an altitude of dream or trance, and behold ourselves crawling uncomfortably about eternity and infinity. Long ago men said that mankind was like an ants' nest, but they did not believe it. Only a theologian said it, and, for joy of an ingenious invention, they repeated it as if it were a reality. But now we can see mankind so. It is not the spaces of the stars that terrify us, but the spaces between one lover and the other, between a child and the dead that bore him. (*MM*, p. 99)

Thomas's own poetry reveals repeated attempts to come to terms with and transcend such alienation. This struggle is conducted on several, interlocking fronts: in the realm of nature, the separation of individual and world is overcome through work; in the realm of society, through language, communication. At the centre of both relations, however, lies that third, all-encompassing context: class.

[138]

This alienation, as we have seen, is lived initially at the level of personal, even sensory experience, and is predicated upon that spectatorial detachment in which we look upon ourselves from an altitude of dream or trance, exiled from the significant moment. It is the predominance of sight over the other senses which reinforces this separation, for sight always posits a gap between observer and observed like that in the poem 'Ambition'. The moments of 'excited significance' and the 'mysterious sensorial life' which interested James and Thomas, on the other hand, are ones in which the whole sensorium is involved, and, momentarily, unified. In 'The Other', the poet sets out to achieve that moment when the suffering, phenomenal self is reunited with its lost ideal essence. It briefly attains one of these 'Moments of everlastingness'. But the journey wasn't really necessary, for the possibility of such a state was implicit from the start, in the very moment of setting out. The poem opens with a synaesthesia which the poet doesn't notice, and, in missing it, he forfeits his chance of revelation there and then. He is glad, we note, not to see but 'To feel the light, and hear the hum / Of bees, and smell the drying grass / And the sweet mint'.

Thomas's poetry is full of this subtle synaesthesia. Memory in *The Childhood* and, as we have seen, in 'Old Man' is associated with smell, and in 'The Word' he speaks of 'the elder scent / That is like food; or . . . / . . . the wild rose scent that is like memory', yet both of these are also associated with a forgetting – of history, of time – in which the self is freed into the mystery of its own living moment. Here even the 'pure thrush word', though it is an 'empty thingless name', takes on a taste, with the bird 'at midday saying it clear / And tart'.

If memory is repeatedly associated with scents, pre-sage for Thomas is defined in terms not of sight but of a sound which remains a physical thing, vibrations of flesh and membrane. In 'The New House' the 'moan' of the wind still recalls its bodily origins, and it 'teases' the ears with a foreboding not 'foreseen' but 'foretold':

> All was foretold me; naught
> Could I foresee;
> But I learned how the wind would sound
> After these things should be.

This substitution of sound and stress for vision is quite deliberate. It extends, for example, to that unforeseen future, where the daylight is blotted out by mist, and the sun shines in vain, so that all sense of limits is lost. And it carries with it too a feeling of powerless-ness and passivity. The self actively foresees nothing. Rather it passively receives what 'was foretold'. Even learning seems a mere passive reception of outside impulses, dependent upon 'how the wind would sound'. The subjunctive here doesn't open up the future as a place of possibility and choice, but as a foreclosed and determined place, yet it is pre*determined* by a force which cannot be pre*dicted*. Nothing is specified about what is foretold (that antithesis of 'all' and 'naught' reinforces the paradox): it is simply 'these things', and their subjective reflex, 'old griefs and griefs / Not yet begun'.

It is because they are unspecified that they cannot be avoided, weigh down with an inexorable power, just as it is the lack of term and definition in those days and nights 'without end' that overwhelms the fragile self. Yet all this is nevertheless dependent upon an act of choice – that act with which the poem opens. For the wind begins to moan as if in response to that shutting of the door. It seems to depend upon the aloneness which makes him feel even a kind of kinship with the house, sharing in its contradictory age and newness. If time is here overthrown it is because vision, the faculty which places the self in control of its context, is also abnegated, just as memory can engulf the self with melancholy because it subverts at the level of such intangibles as smell and touch. The self, that is, in its very sensorium, is subject to contrary pressures, and cannot hold its own identity steady as external impulses merge with internal moods and sensations which also seem to come from somewhere beyond the conscious, vulnerable ego.

'Out in the dark' is centrally a poem about the exposure felt by a subject who feels himself the dream of a dream. It is the lamp of consciousness, 'All the universe of sight', which alone sustains the self. The other senses are party to those external, 'invisible' presences which travel with the fallow fawns and the winds that blow 'Fast as the stars are slow'. Kinesis, motion, sound and touch and invisibility are all linked in this image of a night which drowns all else, which hunts stealthily around but then arrives 'At a swifter bound / Than the swiftest hound'. This bound is soundless, and fear is more felt than heard, the drumming of the blood in the ear, a physical rather than an auditory sensation, 'Drums on my ear / In that sage company drear'. There is here a paradoxical proximity and distance together, 'near, / Yet far', like that in the remarks of Maeterlinck, engulfing both external and internal, light and delight:

> How weak and little is the light,
> All the universe of sight,
> Love and delight,
> Before the might,
> If you love it not, of night.

It is in abandoning the world of sight that the self

succumbs to its inevitable demise, in sleep or death.
Yet, as in 'Lights Out', this is not an unequivocal loss.
Rather it is in abandoning the tyrannous sense of
sight, with all the risks that entails to 'the discursive
intellect' that, as for James, a more authentic and
unitary being can be grasped, in which both inner and
outer realms are transfigured with significance, and
the crude division between the self and the house it
inhabits is overcome. In 'Lights Out', sleep has its
thresholds, 'borders' beyond which all definition merges
into an 'unfathomable deep / Forest' where each track
'Suddenly now blurs'. Significantly, this self is identified
as simultaneously a reading, looking and loving subject, as if the power of print were somehow closely
bound up with the ability to look and value. This association of vision and book is almost unconsciously echoed
in the image of the forest leaves, cloudily blurring
'shelf above shelf' in the last stanza, where the paradox
of hearing a silence again shifts consciousness away
from vision to that more vulnerable threshold sense
where disobedience is impossible. The eyes can shut
against vision and blurring alike; but there is no way
in which the ear can shut out a *silence* which is felt as
an almost tangible presence:

> There is not any book
> Or face of dearest look
> That I would not turn from now
> To go into the unknown
> I must enter, and leave, alone,
> I know not how.
>
> The tall forest towers:
> Its cloudy foliage lowers
> Ahead, shelf above shelf;
> Its silence I hear and obey
> That I may lose my way
> And myself.

Yet this inevitability is the product of a conscious willing. The self is *ready* to abandon book and face, welcomes its solitude. It 'must enter, and leave, alone', but it wilfully obeys that it '*may* lose my way'. This transit is one it makes effortlessly, even though it does not understand it. 'I know not how' indicates the self-division of a subject not in control of itself, whose experience and knowledge are not consonant. He 'cannot choose' not to lose his way, and this indicates just how much the self-directing traveller was 'deceived' even in his conscious, daytime choices of road and track. There is still no way in which the sundered subject can be restored to itself: it can have either the wakeful anguish of consciousness, with all its tasks and warring antitheses, or the sweeter sleep of unconsciousness, but it cannot combine both.

Except, that is, by recovering as James suggested in *Talks to Students* that mysterious sensuous satisfaction derived from hard physical work which endows life with value and which, we have seen, Thomas envied as the birthright of working men and women. In a handful of poems – we have already discussed 'Fifty Faggots' – Thomas caught the pleasures of this bodiliness which for him linked labour and poetry as expressions of a common creative energy. In his prose, he is well aware of its literary sources: 'Carlyle and Whitman, Morris and Tolstoy, have all helped to create a view of those who work with their hands which has already influenced many artists', he wrote in a review (*DC*, 10 April 1909). In the poetry however, appropriately enough, it comes without this cumbersome intellectual baggage, as a fresh thing.

'Sowing', for example, offers a fusion of the senses, so that even the visual is subordinated to a synaesthesia in which it cannot be separated out and thus fragment consciousness. Even the apparently visual image of the

[143]

ground as 'dry . . . / As tobacco-dust' is transformed by the addition of 'sweet', which not only brings out 'dry' as a taste but also releases smell, thus preparing the way for the main verb of the second stanza:

> It was a perfect day
> For sowing; just
> As sweet and dry was the ground
> As tobacco-dust.
>
> I tasted deep the hour
> Between the far
> Owl's chuckling first soft cry
> And the first star.

But it is not taste alone which prevails here. The description of the owl's cry fuses sound and touch in 'soft' and 'chuckling', while the onomatopoeic quality of the latter carries, too, a sense of the actual physical process of making the sound. The words 'deep' and 'far' likewise lead on to the kinetic and tactile fusion in 'long stretched' in the next stanza, while the synaesthesia is rounded off at the end in the appeal to 'hark' (a much more kinetic act than merely hearing) which turns the rain even in its windless lightness into something which touches, as tear and kiss, in a language more intimate than that of speech. The 'good-night' here is a kind of tucking-up after the physical satisfactions of labour. The 'perfect day' is matched by a sense of fullness and completion in the body which has worked itself to a natural conclusion, which can also now stretch in satisfaction like the hour. The planting of the seeds, in its bodily effort, becomes an appropriation of time, too: this sowing has taken purchase on the future, on the seeds of time themselves, and in the process has made past and present alike sites not of loss but of fruition and fulfilment.

[144]

Human actions in 'Digging' transform the world, squaring the mustard field, digging the earth, burning the waste, reclaiming entropy by making the dead useful again. It is therefore appropriate that the last two acts of the poem should contrast human and animal acts. It is not voice, the power of singing, which distinguishes human from animal, but work, the power to alter the world. The hand that crumbles the dark earth is one calloused with its labours. Whereas the robin is locked in repetition, singing over and over again a song repeated every autumn, the mirth which the hearer extracts from its sadness – and the sadness too, which is also a human extraction, like that which releases the various scents – redeems the time by working on the present, turning even its debris to use, constructing the spring by its activities here and now. Thus the 'To-day' with which 'Digging' opens and the sense of temporal succession with which it closes are brought together into a meaningful unity by a consciousness fortified, able to integrate opposites, fix them in their overflowing sufficiency ('It is enough').

As elsewhere, Thomas is divided in his attitude towards the shifting relations between 'mind' and 'nature'. On the one hand, the unreflective creatures of this world share an intuitive wholeness of being from which we are cast out. They are, one might say, 'at home in the world', still in Eden, not divorced from the sensuous immediacy of experience. On the other hand, they cannot forge past, present and future into a imaginative unity of being which characterizes the human, and makes us creatures whose meanings are found, not in the cyclical repetitions of nature, but in the movement of history. Once again, that is, the human is placed at that interface or threshold which, I have argued, internalizes Thomas's intuitive grasp of a social precariousness.

Recalling his childhood, in the same chapter of *The South Country* which provides sources for 'Old Man', Thomas speaks of a time when his encounters with the natural world always had this directness and vivacity:

> In those days we did not see a tree as a column of a dark stony substance supporting a number of green wafers that live scarcely half a year, and grown for the manufacture of furniture, gates, and many other things; but we saw something quite unlike ourselves, large, gentle, of foreign tongue . . . and they were givers of a clear deep joy that cannot be expressed. (p.143)

It is easy to miss the hints here. For what comes between then and now is not just a metaphysical fall from grace. Rather, it is a fall into a quite specific kind of society and a quite specific set of values. The trees were 'givers' of joy; but now, dominated by the commodity values of a culture founded on manufacture, they are defined only in the crudest terms of utility and price. To see the world in a different light restores us to a sense of our own worth too, 'recalls us to times when an account of our physical self, height, width, weight, colour, age, etc., would bear no relation whatever to the true self'. In *The South Country*, Thomas had just been discussing the work of one writer who above all epitomized such an alternative vision, Thomas Traherne, that newly-discovered seventeenth-century mystic whose writings Thomas eagerly reviewed as they appeared in the 1900s. One of Thomas's earliest critics, R. P. Eckert, in *Edward Thomas: A Biography and Bibliography* (1937) had adduced this discussion of Traherne as evidence that Thomas was never caught up in or responded to the 'social changes that seemed to have sprung up, almost overnight, when Edward VII ascended the throne': 'Traherne was of a past generation, out of place in the company of modern social theory' (pp. 86–7). But if, instead of recruiting Thomas to that cult of an apolitical 'nature' which actually sustains a deeply privileged version of England, we try to answer when such whispers bid, we can hear a different story here.

In addition to the reviews and *The South Country*, Thomas returned to Traherne in *Maeterlinck* and *Jefferies*, and his anthology of *Poems and Songs for the Open Air* reprinted a poem which explains his appeal. The poem equates the child's fall from grace with his passage from a world of primitive communism where he 'wandered over all men's grounds', without regard to 'hedges, ditches, limits, bounds', to a world of 'Cursed and devised proprieties', in which all the sins dependent on property, 'envy, avarice / And fraud', overwhelm and dispossess him, dividing joys previously combined. The loss the father feels in 'Old Man' is precisely of a state of awareness like this, still known to his child, which 'Did not divide my joys, but all combine'. It is the same argument Thomas develops in *The South Country*, even citing a passage which recalls 'the same weariness, nay even horror' as of one left alone in the world which engulfs him in that poem.

The key moment in this argument comes when Thomas cites, and comments on, Traherne's excited vision of a world under common ownership, in a logic which transcends that of bourgeois property relations:

That power to create worlds in the mind is the imagination, and is the proof that the creature liveth and is divine . . . 'You never enjoy the world aright . . . till you . . . perceive yourself to be the sole heir of the whole world.' And our inheritance is more than the world, 'because men are in it who are every one sole heirs as well as you.' It is a social mysticism. . . His is the true 'public mind', as he calls it. . .

    Here . . . he seems to advance to the position of Whitman, whom some have blamed for making the word 'divine' of no value because he would apply it to all, whereas to do so is no more than to lay down that rule of veneration for all men – and the other animals – which has produced and will produce the greatest revolutions. (pp. 140–1)

This spiritual revolution is that which, in noticeably Trahernian terms, Thomas experiences briefly in 'The Other', coming home as 'An old inhabitant of earth' to an earth no longer parcelled into private properties, but instead, in defiance of logic, 'Held on an everlasting lease'.

The signs of such a vision are everywhere in Thomas. In 'England', for example, his emphasis on the 'common man' as the true repository of Englishness carries with it an insistence on the diversity of this 'commonwealth', which is quite literally a wealth shared in common. His closing remarks confirm this, taking up the aspersions on gamekeepers and landowners earlier in the essay. Izaak Walton, he says, 'reminds us how much a man may be lord of that he does not possess. He is speaking of some fields which belonged to a rich man with many lawsuits pending, yet he who "pretended no title" to them could take a sweet content in them' (*LS*, p. 110).

His *alter ego* in this same essay also makes a careful distinction between true patriotism, the disinterested buckling-to of ordinary people, and that of capitalists who identify England with their own property. Thomas's droll parenthesis makes it clear he shares the sentiments:

    'If I owned a bit of land I think it might make a great difference to my feelings.' (Here is a chance for a landowner who wants to manufacture patriots.) 'But I don't own any, and in common with the forty-millions of the dispossessed, I know that I am never likely to. The dice are cogged against us by the capitalists and other cunning monopolists, who, in their turn, love no country but only what they own in it.' (*LS*, p. 95)

Ownership is both an absurdity and a disgrace for Thomas, and his recurrent use of the concept of 'No Man's Land', of which Lob is one of the guardians, expresses his deepest convictions about the shamefulness of a property system that dispossesses those forty-millions of their natural birthright. The receding 'Heart of England' is then that terrain described in all its ambiguity in the book of that name, where a disused road which like Lob, is 'disappearing', trodden now only by 'adventurers, lovers, exiles, plain endurers of life' has become 'a grove full of hazels and birds, the innermost kernel of the land, because nobody owns and nobody uses it' (p. 114). The chapter called 'No Man's Garden' gives similar substance to 'No Man', speaking of a twelve-foot strip of grass that runs for a mile along a country road, carrying the traces of tramps:

This is no man's garden. Every one who is nobody sits there with a special satisfaction, watching the swift, addle-faced motorist, the horseman, the farmer, the tradesman, the publican, go by; for here he is secure as in the grave, and even as there free – if he can – to laugh or scoff or wonder or weep at the world.

The old tramp he meets there, after telling him of a murder for ten shillings he committed twenty years before, goes on, in a vein of class resentment, 'indignantly, but with good humour' about '"What a country this is"':

'There are not enough sticks in this wood to warm the only man that wants them. I suppose they use the firing

to keep the pheasants warm. Hark at them! If I was a
rich man I wouldn't keep such birds . . .

'England is not such a place as it was when I was a
young man . . .'

And he concludes: "'No, there is no room in England
now for toe-rags like me and you'".

What the tramp expresses here as an alternative to
private property is a kind of *usufruct*, in which the land
is used by all when they need it but never actually
owned by anybody, and therefore possessed in common
by all. These remarks provide a material base to that
fanciful quotation from Izaak Walton in 'England' and
also link with Thomas's praise for Walter de la Mare's
'truest and least rhetorical of poems on England' in
The English Review in December 1910: 'He has not
bought land, nor inherited, nor rented, nor cultivated,
nor gone out to admire it, but he is the master of an
immeasurable strange tract.' In an early essay in *Rose
Acre Papers* in 1904, Thomas had offered an explicit
version of this usufruct which shows both the radicalism and the limits of what he calls this 'cheerful
communism'. For if it disputes powerfully the right of
the property owner to fence off the land, its whimsical
idealism never actually engages with the hungry
realities of rents, exactions, poverty, preferring instead
to look down superciliously on the barbarity of ownership, while revelling in an impudent, subversive
trespass:

Go when you will – except at the garden party – and you
will see that I alone am lord of the roses and all the
grass. I have sometimes wondered when the 'owner' will
acknowledge my right. Yet I am in no haste to enter into
possession: that in itself would be barbarous . . . I prefer
to be outside, innocently investing the place, never
demanding capitulation or storming the wall. I am well
provisioned with pride, and am content to see the great

[150]

man go in and out, ignorant of rivalry. Never was such
cheerful communism, such wholesome confusion of
meum and *tuum*. (p. 9)

In *The South Country* Thomas tells us that the English
game preserve invites, in an oddly evocative phrase,
'the pleasures of a trespasser's unskilled labour'.
Trespassing may endorse, almost tolerantly, the 'theft'
against which it rebels. But there is no doubt that for
Thomas enclosure is an 'un-English' activity, and the
trespasser not only transgresses in the name of some
future 'communism'; he also asserts a more ancient
'propriety' than that of the present.

The old tramp, Jack Noman, in 'May the Twenty-
third' embodies such a principle. The evasive bonhomie
of the poet's banter refuses either to condone or con-
demn the tramp's petty pilfering of watercress from a
privately owned stream. For Jack, 'ownership' inserts
a set of mystifying relationships into the world. Property
breeds lies. His refusal to lie is also a refusal to
acknowledge the very institution of property, itself
founded on a primal theft. Yet the strategy which
substitutes a mutual giving for the inequities of buying
and selling is only a rationalization, not a denial, of the
actual cash-nexus within which the two drop-outs, poet
and tramp, continue to exist:

> 'Where did they come from, Jack?' 'Don't ask it,
> And you'll be told no lies.' 'Very well:
> Then I can't buy.' 'I don't want to sell.
> Take them and these flowers, too, free.
> Perhaps you have something to give me?'

The poetry abounds in such paradoxical linguistic
inversions of value: 'I should be rich to be so poor'
('Liberty'), 'a poor man of any sort, down to a king'
('The Signpost').

Such a preoccupation is at the centre of a sequence of

poems for his own children in which he explores, with a deliberate delicate *faux-naïveté*, the contradiction between intrinsic and exchange values, between (in the words of the poem 'What will they do?') 'What has great value and no price.' This contradiction between the *private* innocence which reveals a shared world and the *public* system of privatizing relations is explored with a more sceptical irony in 'The Gypsy'. It is the outcast who has most immediate access to an enriching intersubjectivity out- side the cash nexus. But the poem adroitly avoids romanticizing the gypsies as represent-atives of an alternative community to the commercial necromancy of the rural fair, by showing that they too are caught up in the world of 'the golden sovereign' from which, nevertheless, their vagrancy preserves a cautious distance. The tension is sustained throughout the central encounter of poet and gypsy woman, whose flirtatious begging transforms sordid commercial dependency into a kind of contest between equals, a mock auction which parodies that one held in earnest at the end of the poem. 'Luck' here becomes a synonym for a skill, daring and good-fortune that cannot be reduced to the laws of the market – synonymous, in fact, with the 'grace / And impudence in rags' which the enjambment, and the situational irony (importunate mother and child a fortnight before Christmas), endow with religious force:

> 'My gentleman,' said one, 'you've got a lucky face.'
> 'And you've a luckier,' I thought, 'if such a grace
> And impudence in rags are lucky.' 'Give a penny
> For the poor baby's sake.' 'Indeed I have not any
> Unless you can give change for a sovereign, my dear.'
> 'Then just half a pipeful of tobacco can you spare?'
> I gave it. With that much victory she laughed content.

The self-critical irony that points out his own inequitable

surplus, while at the same time laying a trap for the gypsy woman she is adept enough to avoid, charts a relationship in which human values undercut the canny accommodations of the market. Both parties assume a 'profit' from the deal; both in fact receive a benefit from the mutual giving which exceeds any tangible gain. The lurking etymological pun linking 'gratitude' and 'grace' suggests an actual adequation between ineffable human qualities which transcend the cash nexus, qualities which cannot be converted into their 'proper coin' any more than the workmen's grins and the brother's music can be reduced to the ratios of supply and demand:

> I should have given more, but off and away she went
> With her baby and her pink sham flowers to rejoin
> The rest before I could translate to its proper coin
> Gratitude for her grace. And I paid nothing then
> As I pay nothing now with the dipping of my pen
> For her brother's music when he drummed the
>   tambourine
> And stamped his feet, which made the workmen passing
>   grin,
> While his mouth-organ changed to a rascally Bacchanal
>   dance
> 'Over the hills and far away.'

The nursery rhyme tonalities endorse the dissociation of creative giving which confers an elective grace (poem and the music it celebrates alike are offered *gratis*, a kind of grace-saying independent of a consumer) from the market of death which afflicts buyers, sellers and commodities alike. The encounter of poet and nomad has no final price, but grows in worth and estimation with recollection, while the syntax ambiguously reduces men and beasts at the auction to the same status as doomed commodities:

[153]

> This and his glance
> Outlasted all the fair, farmer and auctioneer,
> Cheap-jack, balloon-man, drover with crooked stick, and
>   steer,
> Pig, turkey, goose, and duck, Christmas corpses to be.
> Not even the kneeling ox had eyes like the Romany.

Thomas avoids bucolic sentimentalism in this poem by a sustained ambivalence. If the gypsies embody a set of values in opposition to that of the auction, they nevertheless participate in its venality ('pink sham flowers' predicts 'cheap-jack', 'rascally' is echoed perhaps unconsciously in the lurking metaphor of 'crooked'). If the remorseful poet espouses a similar contempt for the cash nexus, he holds on to his sovereign, and the implication (that there is no 'price' which adequately defines this 'great value') almost seems like a casuistic evasion. The encounter is liberating yet necessarily brief: only in retrospect, detached from any actual communal continuity which might disillusion and dispossess, can the contact blossom into revelation.

The wind of 'Up in the Wind' seems related to that which sweeps across 'the hollow wooded land' of 'The Gypsy', and that which persecutes the poet-solitary in 'Wind and Mist'. The pub Thomas finds by accident up a farm track, in a clump of beeches near a crossroads in the downs is another one of those lost hearts of England, hidden yet homely, to those who know the landscape's secrets. 'It hides from either road, a field's breadth back', and it is the trees you see from the distance, not the house, though the clump is 'homely, too, upon a far horizon / To one that knows there is an inn within'. It is only ironically a 'public house', as the sarcasm of the girl behind the bar, with her unexpected accent, makes clear, in the sudden reported exclamation which plunges us into the poem *in medias res*:

'I could wring the old thing's neck that put it there!
A public house! It may be public for the birds,
Squirrels and such-like, ghosts of charcoal-burners
And highwaymen.' The wild girl laughed. 'But I
Hate it since I came back from Kennington.
I gave up a good place.' Her cockney accent
Made her and the house seem wilder by calling up –
Only to be subdued at once by wildness –
The idea of London there in that forest parlour . . .

These ghosts are precisely the kind of fanciful presence the poet himself has been peopling the landscape with, and she herself at first, with her shriek, her sighing, her flashing eyes and wild hair, seems to have an almost supernatural quality. But this landscape is unpeopled for more material reasons. The roads have fallen into disuse except for the poet, 'A market waggon every other Wednesday, / A solitary tramp, some very fresh one / Ignorant of these eleven houseless miles', and the occasional 'motorist from a distance slowing down / To taste whatever luxury he can'. The place is 'midway between two railway lines / Far out of sight or sound of them'. It is, in fact, economic marginalization which lies behind its desertion. Then as now, paths run on all sides to the inn; but now nobody uses them. But this is not all loss, for the land has reverted to a more ancient seclusion, and the wildness of the girl is, in a sense, in keeping here, making her almost the 'spirit' or, in another version, the 'ghost' of the place, a kind of *genius loci*, just as her 'common' accent links her, at a deeper level, to a time when all the land of England was common:

But the land is wild, and there's a spirit of wildness
Much older, crying when the stone-curlew yodels
His sea and mountain cry, high up in Spring.
He nests in fields where the gorse is free as
When all was open and common. Common 'tis named

And calls itself, because the bracken and gorse
Still hold the hedge where plough and scythe have chased
   them.

(In 'For These' it is men, ironically, who inherit what
nature leaves over, inverting this order of precedence:
'Where what the curlew needs not, the farmer tills.')

The girl's own story tells both of how she came to be
here and how the place became so deserted. The two
tales are intimately related. For her, it seems that her
own private narrative is a chronicle of accidents, like
that which for Thomas himself resulted in his own 'accidentally Cockney nativity'. Yet behind both destinies
lies that whole pattern of demographic shifts which took
both him and her to London, and also brings them back
to this place. She is preoccupied with how –

> 'Twould have been different . . . suppose
> That widow had married another blacksmith and
> Kept on the business. This parlour was the smithy.
> If she had done, there might never have been an inn:
> And I, in that case, might never have been born . . .'

Years ago, this had all been forest, and the smith had
the charcoal burners for company. A man had come
from a beech country in the shires with an engine to cut
the timber, accompanied by a boy to feed the engine.
The man married the smith's widow, who had already
turned the smithy into an alehouse. At this point, the
narrative takes a less impersonal turn, as she '"suppose[s]
they fell in love, the widow / And my great-uncle that
sawed up the timber: / Leastways they married. The
little boy stayed on. / He was my father."'

Behind and through these personal destinies, a larger
fate is unfolding itself. The trees are being cut down to
fuel a growing economy, agriculture initially expands,
to feed a growing urban population ('"It all happened
years ago"' she tells us). In the process work patterns

change and values change with them. Changes in spiritual values, however, are intimately bound up with more material ones, of price and purchase:

> 'My father, he
> Took to the land. A mile of it is worth
> A guinea; for by that time all the trees
> Except those few about the house were gone.
> That's all that's left of the forest unless you count
> The bottoms of the charcoal-burners' fires –
> We plough one up at times . . .'

Her own move to Kennington, for her simply a private adventure, is part of the same collective process, and her return is likewise dictated by economic forces, the need to look after her father ('"I draw the ale and he grows fat," she muttered'). The wind perpetually roaring in the trees then becomes a symbol of this economic destiny, and she projects on to it all the fury and indignation she feels but cannot express in more material terms. A 'thief' (she clearly implies herself), threw the inn's signboard, whose creaking in the wind regularly kept her awake, into the pond, in a minor and symbolic protest against this destiny –

> 'But no one's moved the wood from off the hill
> There at the back, although it makes a noise
> When the wind blows, as if a train were running
> The other side, a train that never stops
> Or ends. And the linen crackles on the line
> Like a woodfire rising.'

For her, unlike the poet, the noise of the train signifies escape, more painful now because it is not the real thing, but perpetually taunts her with what she has given up, the freedom of the city. Yet when the poet asks her about going back to Kennington, she is not only stoical and resigned, she almost seems to choose to stay here, voluntarily accepting her fate:

She bent down to her scrubbing with 'Not me.
Not back to Kennington. Here I was born,
And I've a notion on these windy nights
Here I shall die. Perhaps I want to die here.
I reckon I shall stay. But I do wish
The road was nearer and the wind farther off,
Or once now and then quite still, though when I die
I'd have it blowing that I might go with it
Somewhere distant, where there are trees no more
And I could wake and not know where I was
Nor even wonder if they would roar again.
Look at those calves.'

She has said enough, and the change of subject brings them back to the pastoral moment of two calves wading in the pond, 'Grazing the water here and there and thinking, / Sipping and thinking, both happily, neither long . . . / As careless of the wind as it of us.' Yet in the double vocative of the final line, '"Look at those calves. Hark at the trees again"', a whole history is summed up. The careless content of the animals contrasts with the shared restlessness of the two people. Yet this is 'company' – that word which occurs at key points in the poem – of a kind. Two accidental Cockneys, their lives shaped by a sequence of accidents which began long before they were born, meet for a moment and share a sense of common things – looking at, harkening to, a shared landscape where their lives momentarily converge, as do all paths which run to the inn. For the inn is, after all, like this world when seen by the 'public mind' of a Traherne, 'A public house and not a hermitage'. A man and woman from different classes and cultures meet briefly upon the ground of their common dispossession, speaking a common language. Something more than a mere exchange of words has gone on here. The sexual undercurrent in this momentary sympathy between the two is all the more significant for the taciturnity. This, the first poem Thomas wrote, and one of his finest, already contains all his most distinctive features. It compacts into a brief space an individual narrative which has the generations behind it. It links the personal and the historic at the moment that its narrator disengages himself wilfully from the pressures of a world he wants to turn his back on. It reminds us, and him, that we are never outside history. And it does all this with an economy of means as quietly reproachful as the girl's own stubborn understatement. The most effective device for achieving this sense of common things lies in the poem's deployment of dialogue, which prevents the poet himself from disappearing into his own self-absorbed reveries, just as, at the beginning, the girl's shriek draws him out of his musing. It is to this aspect of Thomas's poetry that we should now turn our attention.

For all the poet's anxiety about being an 'isolate self-considering brain', few collections of verse can have as many narratives of conversation and encounter, more vocatives, reported speech, or direct celebrations of the unique quiddity and otherness of other creatures and people. Significantly, it is in his article on William Morris in *The Bookman* in February 1911 that Thomas sets out a formula for such a poetic. Chaucer, he says there, as man and poet, was 'social and not isolated' offering 'not an individual but a corporate view of life'. 'In the changed world of the Reformation no writer shows this social quality except the maker of street ballads'. Even Shakespeare 'stands apart from his age in a kind of inevitable exile'. Increasingly, poets are 'unnoticed spectators standing on the outside or at the edge of the life which they record'. Shelley 'ended with a feeling, something like paralysis, due to the total lack of communion with an audience'. What the modern poem conspicuously lacks is a narrative impetus such as Morris sought to supply, for 'the sense of action is dead or atrophied among moderns'. Without a 'generally known' subject matter, 'the work of a race or class as much as of a man', he says, 'narrative perishes, while the lyric composed in solitude for reading in solitude survives.'

He reverts, here, to points made as early as 1901, in the article 'The Lyric Muse' (*DC*, 27 August 1901), where he writes of the Romantics' paradoxical cult of the drama at just the moment that the lyric engulfed all other poetic forms. This, he says, is the mode which 'will prosper, at least so long as individualism makes way in literature', because 'increasing complexity of thought and emotion will find no such outlet as the myriad-minded lyric, with its intricacies of form'. In the two articles, ten gruelling years apart, Thomas exposits the contradiction at the heart of his own poetic. On the one hand, the lyric offers a particular point of view on to a reality too vast and complex to comprehend in full: it foregrounds the individual as the experiential centre of the world. But it also records the individual's marginalization in relation to all those other centres and circumferences with which it overlaps. In this way, he says in 'The Lyric Muse', a lyric poet's 'sense even of common things is so poignant that it must be unique'.

The analogy Thomas uses to explain this relation between unique and common, individual and social, remains only half expounded:

> Everyone must have noticed, standing on the shore, when the sun or moon is over the sea, how the high way of light on the water comes right to his feet, and how those on the right and on the left seem not to be sharing his pleasure, but to be in darkness.

The image is developed in his 1905 review of Ford

Maddox Hueffer's *The Soul of London* (*The Speaker*, 3 June 1905). Hueffer's work attempts, he says, in its narrative stance to find some middle ground between an ideal, synoptic vision and a centreless plurality of individual viewpoints. 'Although seraphic intelligences, on some eminence, may see London as one mighty form and mind, yet to most of us, London is not one but many.' Hueffer avoids generalizations 'dangerously divided from the experience and visions out of which they spring' by arranging several individual points of view into an ensemble, to suggest, but not directly depict, the common ground of all. He does this by suggesting a continuity of public and private, 'the sense of an horizon, of something beyond, *i.e.*, the countless and changing crowd and the few faces in it which we know'. He thus links dialectically the multitude of 'special views' with 'the absolute thing which many different people see in so many different ways' where they intersect. Thomas concludes his review by reverting to that lunar analogy used five years earlier, almost word for word, but with a rider which brings out its significance:

> We think, at first, that it shines for us alone, and makes a bridge over which our dreams alone may travel. But it comes thus to everyone! So it is with all things that move men.

One of the two poems called 'An Old Song' picks up this metaphor, without spelling out the implications outlined here. The whole poem is about perception: the sea 'Was like a mirror shaking', the shore seems a *tabula rasa* 'Where tide had smoothed and wind had dried / The vacant sand' (an image used in 'The sun used to shine' for mind and memory). But into this vacancy a light can break:

> A light divided the swollen clouds
> And lay most perfectly
> Like a straight narrow footbridge bright
> That crossed over the sea to me;
> And no one else in the whole world
> Saw that same sight.

Yet the elation which accompanies this is only ostensibly solitary and exclusive. For it is expressed in terms of a collective lyric, the sea-shanty 'I'll go no more a-roving', a 'sailors' song of merry loving' which slowly forces its way into Thomas's poem until in the penultimate stanza it overwhelms it, turning from refrain to dominant text. The lewdness of the song is then 'far outweighed / By the wild charm the chorus played', and in breaking into this chorus the solitary singer calls up those ghosts of a lost collectivity for whom the individual was simply the lead voice in a group composition. In the same way, in that other poem called 'An Old Song', the 'Lincolnshire Poacher's' glee in trespassing and poaching, roaming 'where nobody had a right but keepers and squires', brings the lonely self, 'at home or anywhere', back into a community which combines strangeness and familiarity in 'a strange kind of delight', so that he is 'for a moment made a man that sings out of his heart'.

Both dialogue and the shift from lead voice to chorus exemplify the folk song's easy transition from individual to public perspective. Reviewing Cecil Sharp's *English Folk Songs*, Thomas stressed this social dimension as something which distinguishes folk from literary lyric, noting 'That social composition without any individual's work to start on was common under conditions where all men's lives were social is clear'. Folk songs are collective creations – 'they bear the mark of one genius, but it is, surely, the genius of the multitude'. Even their rhythms may be dictated by an ethos of communal work (as in the sea shanty):

[162]

There is more than an echo of the origin in choral dances when we find men and women unable to sing these folk-songs except at some occupation as breaking stones or kneading dough; when lines are repeated as they would be by a singing company. (*DC*, 23 January 1908)

The folk song, then, is social in content, authorship, and delivery, emerging, as he wrote in a review of *The Popular Ballad*, from 'those compact communities where a man could not even think himself separate and independent' (*MP*, 23 December 1907). What interests Thomas, however, is the moment of separation between individual voice and community. In discussing folk song in *The South Country* he singles out several songs in which the individual voice is neither totally absorbed in nor totally detached from its social base, so that although 'composed by the folk', in some small touches they 'reveal the stamp of individuals', adding an extra flourish that witnesses to the 'hand of one man who stands out by himself' (p. 245–9).

This dialectic of individual and social preoccupies Thomas in his criticism. A 1907 review, for example, speaks of 'the inability to bring things *sub specie aeternitatis*' as the reflex of a divided society where 'a writer has enough to do if he does not go beyond the confines of one country, or class, or of himself' (*DC*, 29 October 1907). Yet what he sought in his poetry is the scope and ease, at once 'literary' and 'popular', that he admired in the 'peasant' poet Burns, whose poems, he observes in *Feminine Influences*, 'seem almost always to be the immediate fruit of a definite and particular occasion', but 'are not solitary poetry' because 'They suggest instantly two persons, the lover, the beloved' (pp. 293–4).

The characteristic moment in Thomas's poems is one

[163]

of brief encounter and dialogue like that in 'Up in the Wind', which does go beyond the confines of one class, and suggests how, at the heart of a shared language, lies the image of what an authentically democratic community might be. In 'The Lyric Muse' he had written that 'Democracy has brought with it a discovery more important than that all men are equal; and that is, that all men are different'. By the time he came to write the poetry, he had seen that difference is the very foundation of equality, and equality of difference. Variations on the word 'Equal' recur too frequently in his poems not to have a personal significance (it is not a particularly 'poetic' word). Even when (as in 'Health', 'These things the poets said' and 'Words') the meaning is not political, it nevertheless carries some of the valency to be found in 'Parting'. There too the word is initially used neutrally ('Remembered joy and misery / Bring joy to the joyous equally; / Both sadden the sad'). But the play of equality and difference here leads on to a sharper usage, in which the past, in a kind of ghostly mockery, becomes that democratic utopia which most men place in the future:

> The Past is a strange land, most strange . . .
> Men of all kinds as equals range
> The soundless fields and streets of it.

This recalls that other poem of strange solitudes and ghostly emotions, 'Tears', with its hounds 'not yet combed out, / But still all equals in their rage of gladness', the shortlived equality then transferred to the young countrymen in uniform, soon to be combed out themselves by enemy fire.

There is a moment in *The South Country* where Thomas's exasperation with the vapidity of contemporary élite literature finds him looking hopefully towards popular culture for alternative models, in a way which explains the frequency with which folk songs are copied, echoed or quoted in his own poetry:

> Can it possibly give a vigorous impulse to a new school of poetry that shall treat the life of our time and what in past times has most meaning for us as freshly as those ballads did the life of their time? It is possible; and it is surely impossible that such examples of simple, realistic narrative shall be quite in vain. (p. 246)

A review in the same year spoke of the 'separation of the artist from the common man' and discerned in Yeats's work a form which reconciles them, and 'combines the beautiful simplicity of language, the rich tales, and sometimes the ballad forms of the people with a subtlety of feeling for which there is no parallel in any other age' (*DC*, 5 March 1909).

It is not to the ballad so much as the folk song, however, that Thomas's own poetry turns for a model, for the typical pattern of experience which the song captures is that brief encounter, often at dawn, between one person or another heading in opposite directions. Thomas's 'Early one morning in May I set out' is a fine pastiche of this tradition, substituting a brief class encounter for the erotic one which these songs often contain, focused in one line of direct greeting: 'A gate banged in a fence and banged in my head. / "A fine morning, sir," a shepherd said.' The shepherd may make this a pastoral; but as Thomas's draft versions indicate (he crosses out 'strange carter' and 'scavenger'), it is the greeting across a class divide which counts for him. In the same vein, the insouciant poverty of 'The Huxter' is endorsed by its folkish refrain, 'This fine May morning', and the sombre creatureliness of game-keeper and victims in 'The Gallows' is reinforced by its ballad measures and repetitions. But it is, perhaps, the consummate understatement of the song 'Tonight' which shows Thomas at his best, as a poet who could efface himself completely and allow the new proletariat of the city, living in no ancient way, to speak for themselves in measures which insist on their continuity with the rural past. The delicate but resilient arcadianism and the modest carnality of the poem speak for themselves:

> Harry, you know at night
> The larks in Castle Alley
> Sing from the attic's height
> As if the electric light
> Were the true sun above a summer valley:
> Whistle, don't knock, tonight.
>
> I shall come early, Kate:
> And we in Castle Alley
> Will sit close out of sight
> Alone, and ask no light
> Of lamp or sun above a summer valley:
> Tonight I can stay late.

This experiment with folk song and idiom is couched as a dialogue, but a narrative can also be read between the gaps of its two separate utterances. Among his censures of Hardy's poetry, Thomas reserved special praise for one important feature:

Many of the poems are narratives. Even when lyrical they suggest a chain of events. They are full of understandings, forebodings, memories, endings, questionings. (*MP*, 9 December 1909)

In 'using a lyric stanza . . . for a narrative full of conversation' Hardy has introduced virtually a new genre, he suggests. This form, intermediate between private lyric and public folk song, which might be called a 'narrative lyric' offered opportunities that could be

[166]

developed to fit Thomas's own requirement, in *George Borrow*, for 'narratives that should suggest and represent the continuity of life. [The narrator] could pause for description or dialogue or reflection without interrupting this stream of life' (p. 168). It provides an accurate description of the form Thomas was to employ himself, in poems such as 'Up in the Wind', 'Wind and Mist', 'As the team's head-brass', 'Man and Dog'. But if the model was already implicit in Hardy, it took the further stimulus of Robert Frost's example to mobilize his own poetic gift.

Thomas's correspondence shows a recurrent interest in the dialogue technique. In an early letter to E. S. P. Haynes (15 April 1900), now in the Berg Collection, New York Public Library, of the novel they planned to write jointly, he confessed: 'Dialogue will be my difficulty. If I do it at all, the most important speeches will have to be autobiographical, in which I am least bad.' A letter to Gordon Bottomley four years later regrets his inability to write 'imaginary conversations': 'When a person talks with me there are two monologues to be heard, not one dialogue' (*LGB*, p. 61). By the time the poetry came to be written, Thomas had overcome this more than incidental incapacity, in a way which is highly revealing about both his personal and his literary development. A postcard to Robert Frost in 1914 (now in Dartmouth College Library) shows him interested enough to make suggestions for improving Frost's use of dialogue in one poem, while the essay 'The Stile' in *Light and Twilight* makes an authentic dialogue between man and man the source of an almost visionary liberation from constraint:

> There was no knowing whose was any one thought, because we were in electrical contact and each leapt to complete the other's words, just as if some poet had chosen to use the form of an eclogue and had made us the

two shepherds who were to utter his mind through our dialogue. (pp. 46–51)

Such a sparking, one notes, carries with it an ultra-democratic charge, creating 'an immortal company, where I and poet and lover and flower and cloud and star were equals, as all the little leaves were equal ruffling before the gusts, or sleeping and carved out of the silentness'.

The 'I' of Thomas's poems is rescued, on many occasions, from being a disembodied ghost, by the very fact of encounter and dialogue in a common world. In 'As the team's head-brass' he would actually be trodden down if the ploughman didn't turn his horses; in 'The Mill-Pond' he is startled and then angry at a girl who calls out 'Take care' as he dangles his feet in the stream, until the storm bursts and he has to crouch for shelter, knowing her 'Beautiful and kind, too'. Very often, his exchanges are of this kind, abrupt and per-functory, and yet suggesting a whole world of unspoken meanings, as in the one terse exclamation at the heart of 'House and Man' – '"Lonely!" he said. "I wish it were lonely"' – or the 'sideways muttered' response, '"Happy New Year, and may it come fastish, too,"' of 'the one man I met up in the woods / That stormy New Year's morning' in 'The New Year'.

The conversation at the heart of 'It was upon' is a single short sentence, half empty greeting, without reply, yet it acts as a pivot for the whole movement of the poem, setting up a multitude of perspectives radiating from, and converging upon, a spot fortuitously singled out by the momentary exchange:

> It was upon a July evening.
> At a stile I stood, looking along a path
> Over the country by a second Spring
> Drenched perfect green again. The lattermath

[168]

Will be a fine one.' So the stranger said,
A wandering man. Albeit I stood at rest,
Flushed with desire I was. The earth outspread,
Like meadows of the future, I possessed.

And as an unaccomplished prophecy
The stranger's words, after the interval
Of a score years, when those fields are by me
Never to be recrossed, now I recall,
This July eve, and question, wondering
What of the lattermath to this hoar Spring?

Poet and stranger stand in a kind of mirror relation,
each of them advancing into a future which is the
other's past. Looking along the path is for the poet a
prospect forward in time as well as space. 'Possessed' is
a strategically placed verb, surrounding those meadows
of the future with the first person singular so that,
syntactically, he seems to encompass his destiny. Yet
there is asymmetry here too, for the question of the last
line seems like an answer to the other's remark, which
has taken twenty years to form. Unanswered, it leaves
us, as successors to that 'wandering man', ourselves
on the point of departure for a new and unknown
destination.

The stranger's lattermath (a late mowing or reaping) lies in the opposite direction to the poet's, and
may well have been accomplished. His perspective now
complements that of twenty years ago, for he now looks
back across the fields of time which then, as the octet
closed, he was about to cross. The poem enacts the
rhythms of prolepsis and nostalgia, surging forward
with desire, yearning backwards after the attenuated
recall that comes so belatedly in the final sentence,
then briskly, yet without hope, turning to 'question,
wondering' the new future which points, through spring,
towards winter, not summer. The nostalgia is not just

for the lost future or the abandoned past, but also for the lost inexplicable mystery of the wandering man, who now seems like some remote presentiment of his own present self, a ghostly double invested retrospectively with subversive power. The encounter, hingeing on one moment itself then framed by a further moment of *pentimento* twenty years on, creates a complex narrative tension, like that which Thomas describes in a poem of Hardy's: 'The form is a sonnet, and if it is in a sense "a moment's monument", the moment is full of years, and it is an implied narrative' (*MP*, 9 December 1909). In miniature, it enshrines, too, the archetypal pattern of Thomas's poetry, a brief, enigmatic exchange between strangers, charged with yet withholding significance.

The interdependence and mutuality of selves is a recurring theme of Thomas's poetry, but it is usually accompanied by a sense of effort, of obstruction, of a meaning not fully communicated or understood in the exchanges between people. Yet the perception of mutuality is a radical one.

A review of 1909 refers to Shelley's remarks on 'the influence of other minds . . . in transforming a visible object before it is taken down into the alembic of the spirit', and quotes the letter to Mary Godwin which claims 'My mind, without yours, is dead and cold as the dark midnight river when the moon is down' (*DC*, 9 December 1909). What seems of importance in this use of a recurring image is the vacuity which arises in the subject deprived of the ratifying presence of another.

The poem for Thomas's father, 'P.H.T.', seems to recall that 'deathly solemnity' which in *The Childhood* Thomas associated with church and Sunday under the paternal gaze. Its stark initials are almost already an epitaph on a headstone, though it merely looks forward to the father's death. The patriarchal 'omnipotence' of

the aloof spectator in 'Ambition', who half believed he
'had made the loveliness of prime, / Breathed its life
into it and were its lord, / And no life lived save this
'twixt cloud and rime', here gives way to a soberer
recognition both of the reality of other men and of the
'spaces . . . between a child and the dead that bore him'.
The 'ambition' to be 'omnipotent' of that poem is here
castrated into impotence – a state which, in their
mutual estrangement, seems to inflict father and son:

> I may come near loving you
> When you are dead
> And there is nothing to do
> And much to be said.

> To repent that day will be
> Impossible
> For you, and vain for me
> The truth to tell.

> I shall be sorry for
> Your impotence:
> You can do and undo no more
> When you go hence,

> Cannot even forgive
> The funeral.
> But not so long as you live
> Can I love you at all.

The father does and undoes, as the train in 'Ambition'
creates and then destroys the mood of that poem. If
death reduces him to 'impotence', it is noticeable that,
as in 'Ambition', the poet still cannot utter what should
be said. Both repentance for the father and truth-telling
for the son are thus denied, like the telling and knowing
of 'Ambition'. There is a kind of double castration of

speech. The return of the ending mocks the failure of reciprocity it describes.

'No one so much as you' is more complex still in its movement, discriminating degrees of response, but aware, too, of a discrepancy, a disproportion, in the relationship, revealed not only in the gap between insight and reticence, but between thinking and feeling, accepting and responding. Following Helen Thomas's lead, many critics have seen this as a poem about his mother rather than his wife, to the extent that George Thomas, in his variorum edition of *The Collected Poems*, without any authority except 'Helen Thomas's statement to me that the poem was about the poet's mother', retitles it 'M.E.T.', on the analogy with the poem to his father. One can see why, in its sad denials of love, the poem could be distressing to a devoted widow and embarrassing to sympathetic and grateful critics. But the assumption belies all the evidence of biography, including *The Childhood* and George Thomas's own *Edward Thomas: A Portrait*, which makes it clear that the feeling of the son for the mother was unusually direct and unforced. It also goes against the textual evidence of the poem. For the lines 'You are not bold' even negatively, and 'And could not burn' are more appropriate to a wife than a mother, and, if he contemplates burying his father, there is no reason why a mother should survive him, as the opening stanza envisages. Most importantly, though, the last two stanzas seem to hint at those speculations about divorce which George Thomas dismisses (p. 232), one suspects for the same reasons of respectability that led him to credit Helen's belief, Moore to drop the reference to revolution, and any number of critics to talk about 'timeless rural communities' without ever looking at what Thomas himself said, at times in anger and indignation as well as admiration, about the lives of the rural poor. But this is to substitute hagiography for criticism. It does a disservice to the honesty with which Thomas confronted his own predicament, and, most important of all, it significantly reduces the scope and power of this poem, which in the end forges a new and positive feeling out of all these negatives, writing the kind of 'love poem' which in its cautious, sceptical candour eschews all rhetoric and insincerity.

'And you, Helen' speaks of wishing to return to his wife all that she has given him, but there is a baffling, frustrating sense of inhibition: he cannot return to her her own identity, any more than he can give her himself, in return for her own gift of self. Yet he is not even sure, as that double qualification with which the poem ends indicates, that this would be a satisfactory gift, since, in the inability to give himself to another, he is cut off from discovering what the real nature of this self is. The failure of reciprocation results in a suppression of inner authenticity:

> I would give you youth,
> . . . all you have lost
> Upon the travelling waters tossed,
> Or given to me. If I could choose
> Freely in that great treasure-house
> Anything from any shelf
> I would give you back yourself,
> And power to discriminate
> What you want and want it not too late,
> . . . And myself, too, if I could find
> Where it lay hidden and it proved kind.

Unable to give his own self, he necessarily withholds hers from her, so that each is constantly in danger of being lost in the tumult and confusion of the moment, the 'dark moonless river' which, so frequently in Thomas, is associated with desolation and excommunication.

Yet again, the poem itself seems a kind of return gift

[173]

which absolves the guilt at expropriating, without
return, another self. In 'Rain', a similar lament for a
'solitude' in which all loves have drowned becomes, in
the moment of despair, a celebration which reaches out
to recover and endorse those supposedly lost loves:

> Blessed are the dead that the rain rains upon:
> But here I pray that none whom once I loved
> Is dying tonight or lying still awake
> Solitary, listening to the rain,
> Either in pain or thus in sympathy
> Helpless among the living and the dead,
> Like a cold water among broken reeds,
> Myriads of broken reeds all still and stiff,
> Like me who have no love which this wild rain
> Has not dissolved except the love of death . . .

The notion of sympathy complicates, and releases the
potential of, the symbolism, syntactically confusing
the analogy of the myriad of isolate broken selves with
a suggestion that they are the single current of the cold
water, of which he too may be part. 'Independence',
Thomas noted in *Rose Acre Papers*, 'commonly means a
state in which we never know on whom we depend'
(p. 125). These poems chart an obscure intuition of
that interdependence that underlies isolation.

The metaphor of the poem recurs in an observation
which makes this movement through solitude to sympathy an explicit one, in *Walter Pater*:

A man cannot say all that is in his heart to a woman or
another man. The waters are too deep between us. We
have not the confidence in what is within us, nor in our
own voices. Any man talking to the deaf or in darkness
will leave unsaid things which he could say were he not
compelled to shout, or were it light. (p. 208)

Behind this lies the dispersal of the close intimacies

and face-to-face contact of traditional community into the massed solitudes of urban aggregation which the poem 'I built myself a house of glass' records. In the construction of these spaces between men, the self paradoxically finds itself destroyed by the independence it desired. The fragmentations of a class society ('tenement/Or palace') do not even provide the security which might at least be expected as the return for isolation. In the transparency and brittleness of the constructed ego, anguish actually increases. Separation intensifies exposure:

> I built myself a house of glass:
> It took me years to make it:
> And I was proud. But now, alas!
> Would God someone would break it.
>
> But it looks too magnificent.
> No neighbour casts a stone
> From where he dwells, in tenement
> Or palace of glass, alone.

The dissociation is not just between people but within them, between self as subject and as object, agent and patient. The greatest obstacle to the liberation for which each yearns lies in the inability to imagine that the other suffers the same anguish and the same yearning – the indecision that lies at the heart of 'What will they do?' – so that none dares throw the first stone that all desire.

But the insulation of the lyric voice can facilitate a candour that a more public art inhibits. To assume another who corresponds to oneself, and to speak to this merely putative 'ghostly double', with a frankness concerned only to 'get it right' in words, may be to call up a responsive voice:

But the silence of solitude is kindly; it allows a man to speak as if there were another in the world like himself;

[175]

> and in very truth, out of the multitudes, in the course of
> years, one or two may come, or many, who can enter that
> solitude and converse with him, inspired by him to
> confidence and articulation. (*Pater*, p. 208)

This other is not cut off from the multitude, but is its
envoy, a link man who ensures a continuity between
private and public discourse. He is a representative
other, not because he is an 'average man', but because
his exceptional nature reaffirms that an authentic
social relationship is at least possible. He mediates
between first and third persons, opening up the circuit
between self and world.

Thomas is speaking here of the relationship between
poet and reader: to read a poem is to enter into another
man's 'ego-rhythms', the essential forms of his identity.
But the same pattern recurs within the internal structure of Thomas's poems, where a self-conscious and
isolated self reaches hesitantly towards engagement,
in love, work, conversation, with another:

> In the best work, personality, bred of intellectual sincerity
> and strength, is so powerful, though it may also be
> vague, or, as in Shakespeare, exceedingly complex, that
> the reader loses himself for a moment, just as when he
> realizes the distinct nature of another man, by looking
> suddenly with unwonted clearness into his eyes. (*DC*,
> 4 July 1904)

Such is the pattern of 'That girl's clear eyes'; but to
reach the point of saying this is something, and it is
this dual movement, in which a recording of isolation
undercuts the singularity of the dereliction, that con-
stitutes the 'confidence and articulation' of Thomas's
poetry. 'What will they do?' seems another chronicle
of abandonment; but it rehearses, too, a dependency
which, in being acknowledged, allows another discovery.
The poem opens with a tentative questioning that
shifts at once into a self-dismissive certainty:

[176]

What will they do when I am gone? It is plain
That they will do without me as the rain
Can do without the flowers and the grass
That profit by it and must perish without.
I have but seen them in the loud street pass;
And I was naught to them. I turned about
To see them disappearing carelessly.
But what if I in them as they in me
Nourished what has great value and no price?
Almost I thought that rain thirsts for a draught
Which only in the blossom's chalice lies,
Until that one turned back and lightly laughed.

The sustaining analogy itself turns back and laughs, as it unfolds its own latent contradiction. Explicitly, it proposes a one-way dependence. Just below the surface hovers a metaphor from mercantilist economics, rising to visibility in the words 'profit' and 'price', of a commercial transaction in which one man's gain must be another's loss. The flowers seem to be unproductive beneficiaries of the rain's gratuitous charity: he presents himself as the ungrateful and unresponsive recipient of others' bounty.

At the same time, he is guilty, and yet feels neglected. It is they who 'spend' nothing on him, disappear 'carelessly'. If he 'was naught to them', he, on the contrary invests them with a love that issues from his need, which endows them with unique value, so that his guilt is unnecessary. 'Carelessly' is equivocally placed, qualifying either 'disappearing' or 'turned about', in order to suggest that, after all, his 'care' may appear equally 'careless' to others. Just as the carelessness of one may mirror that of the others, so the line 'But what if I in them as they in me' suggests that the care he reveals may also be reproduced, unknown to him, in the others.

'Value' is outgoing, a spending of the self in love, but it is also intrinsic, an inner quality and worth uncovered by this love, so that it may be mutually enhancing. 'Profit' is selfish, seeking one-sided advantage at the expense of the other: it seals off the self in isolation. 'Value' grows, is nourished, in the two-way exchange in which it is given and received. 'Price' reduces things to the status of a commodity, with a finite worth (there comes a time when it is more profitable to exchange than to retain). It is extrinsic, negotiable. The analogy hindered the recognition of a possibly mutual need by segregating the poet from those others – rain is an overflowing plenitude which is untouched by the privations of the flower.

It is a deeply ambiguous ending. If the other turns, he cannot be 'disappearing carelessly'. The laugh may not be of contempt but of recognition, as the other is startled to see a reflection of his own need in the poet. The possibility of contact has at least been raised in that brief exchange of glances, though it is qualified by a suspicion too deep to be easily dismissed. The glance may not be a confirmation of ostracism but a lost opportunity to alter that condition, foiled by a protective paranoia.

There is a kind of distancing in the narration which leaves open the precise identity of this other who turns back and lightly laughs. It seems as if it might be a quasi-sexual exchange, between man and woman. But this would not explain why, earlier, the poet speaks of 'them' (it is hardly a poem about promiscuity). A letter to Robert Frost which contains the germ of this poem places it as a class encounter, and suggests that what he most admired in Frost's volume *North of Boston*, what in fact made it 'one of the most revolutionary books of modern times', was precisely this ability to confront, and cross, that class gulf which divides one

[178]

individual from another, through a poetry of encounter and dialogue that speaks the demotic tongue:

> I go on writing something every day, sometimes brief unrestrained impressions of things lately seen, like a drover with six newly shorn sheep in a line across a cool woolyard on market morning and me looking back to envy him and him looking back at me for some reason which I can't speculate on. Is this *North of Bostonism*? (19 May 1914; now in Dartmouth College Library)

It is then the estrangement of intellectual and worker that provides the first impulse for this poem, as it does for the first poem he wrote, 'Up in the Wind'. The subsequent generalization, the vagueness even, with which 'they' are defined in 'What will they do?' has a dual function. It universalizes the sense of separation; but it also evades the precise pain of the original recognition, and thus transforms a social and changeable condition into an irremediable metaphysical dilemma. It is the movement, of course, that most of Thomas's critics like, who find uncongenial the suggestion that for him, as he said of William Morris (*SC*, p. 117):

> poetry was not, as it has tended more and more to be in recent times, a matter as exclusive as a caste. He was not half-angel or half-bird, but in all that he did a man on close terms with life and toil, with the actual troublous life of every day, with toil of the hands and brain together . . .

Edna Longley does not reproduce this comment in her selection, *A Language Not To Be Betrayed* (pp. 37–9); and she omits from the *Bookman* essay the stress on art as '"a necessary part" of every man's productive labour', as she omits Thomas's comment, 'He was a faithful Socialist'. She does however cite the remark that Morris 'cared . . . for the arts and crafts and for the

[179]

"shabby hell" of the city and he did not think or find the two cares incompatible, but rather insisted that they were one' – the passage which leads up to his praise of 'The March Wind' for leaving 'the division . . . healed in a beautiful union between love of one woman and of the world'. Yet it is in the nexus between the political and personal passions that this division could be healed in Thomas's poetry too. This implicitly political dimension establishes a link between his love poems and his poems about labourers, land, and work. As Thomas himself says in *A Literary Pilgrim*, Morris's 'humanity of this world' is the source of his 'earth-feeling'; it is what makes the earth "'his delight, his joy, his refuge, his home'".

George Thomas's extremely detailed biography contains only two perfunctory references to Morris (one about the wallpaper at Wick Green) and omits all allusion to the (surely biographically significant?) remark, in 1908, in Professor Thomas's own edition of the *Letters to Gordon Bottomley*: 'Except William Morris there is no other man whom I would sometimes like to have been, no other writing man . . . & isn't [the *Message of the March Wind*] a noble piece of humanity?' (p. 158). Silence is golden, however, compared with the jibing rant of John Moore's about the 'well-meaning cranks' (vegetarians of course) from Bedales School (where Helen taught) that Thomas consorted with at Wick Green –

> inclined to a superior and ladylike Socialism; but they had never experienced the rough fellowship of workers in a pub. They disapproved of luxury and riches; but none of them had ever been hungry or poor. They believed in hygiene, brown bread, the *Manchester Guardian*, William Morris, arts and crafts, folk-dancing, and fresh air . . . They possessed earnest and refined and hygienic wives who held similar views and organized meetings in support of Votes for Women. (pp. 160–1)

We know the type, and we superior Thomas lovers would not dream of having them on our visiting list. Though, strangely, as Moore admits, the (vegetarian) Thomas did.

Yet Thomas *was* concerned with 'the actual, troublous life of every day and toil of the hands and brain together'. And this last phrase, in context, relates not only to his Tolstoyan poems about digging and sowing and cutting wood. It also calls up a specifically socialist goal, set out in the constitution of, for example, the Labour Party, founded in 1900, and many trades unions: 'to secure for the workers by hand and brain the full fruits of their labours'. *Rest and Unrest*, the volume which contains some of the most powerful prose Thomas wrote, including the essay I have cited on several occasions in this study, 'Mothers and Sons', has still not been republished in a modern reprint, though much of the hackwork such as *A Literary Pilgrim in England* has been. (The latter Thomas referred to deprecatingly as *"Omes and 'Aunts'*.) In 'Mothers and Sons' Thomas makes it clear that his sense of a language not to be betrayed finds its true home and authenticating source among the English-speaking working classes of Wales, whose nightingales, he told us in 'Words', have no wings. In that essay he first of all seeks a vision of solitary harmony like those vouchsafed in 'The Other' and in 'Ambition'.

But it cannot be held for more than a moment, any more than they can, and on its dissolution in the cold grey of dawn it seems not only a foolish intoxication but a mockery of the squalor he finds in the Welsh valleys below, when he wakes to see a dark hollow land, 'black and sinister' chimneys, and an earth made 'invalid, pathetic, and bereaved' by industrialization. The village he comes to is despoiled, its river polluted, its people, he feels, degraded, by the changeover from an agricultural to an industrial economy. Yet it is the narrator's own sentimentality, with its Wildean flamboyance, which receives the full weight of the prose's indignation:

> As I walked past the shops, neither urban nor rustic, entirely new and as glaring as possible, but awkward, without tradition and without originality, I was full of magnificent regrets. I ought to have had a mantle of tragic hue to swathe myself in mysterious and haughty woe and to flutter ineffable things in the wind, as I trod the streets that were desolate to me.

In contrast with the 'raptures of regret about the growth of the village' in which the narrator and the poet he visits 'complained together', Thomas sets the speech of the Owens, a working-class family into whose home he is invited. The melody of their speech fulfils, as a social activity, that harmony he had experienced earlier as a private vision set apart from any imaginable universe of discourse. A common language provides the matrix for the individual voices, each with its own peculiar grace. Language here is simultaneously personal and social, for, though the harmony transcends its individual voices, it enhances their individuality. It represents for Thomas an epitome of the authentic community which redeems the self from unproductive isolation, and sustains it against the encroachments of alienating and divisive economic forces:

> Admirable as they were apart they made an indescribable harmony together. Sometimes all talked at once ... Sometimes one told a tale and all attended. Sometimes the talk travelled mysteriously from one to another, and to and fro and crosswise, as if some outside power had descended invisible in their midst and were making a melody out of their lips and eyes, a melody which, I think, never ceased in their hearts.

These people are 'fearless' – Thomas's recurrent value-word to describe the spiritual quality of 'the people':

The father spoke his thoughts and the boy his, and there was nothing which anyone of them would have said or secretly laughed at with his companions which they would not say before all.

Here what was hidden stands revealed for the first time, in a language not to be betrayed, as a social mystery: the hope of an authentic community, embodied already in this class which is to inherit the earth:

> I was disturbed . . . at all this gaiety in the heart of the village darkness, partly because I was unable to see why it should exist, and as foolishly sure that there would never be an end to the darkness unless it eclipsed this gaiety in a revolution of some kind – impious thought and unpardonable if it had not been vain. That gaiety cannot be quenched.

Any renovation of poetic language requires a cultural revolution, he implies, that would realign the poet with a community of this kind, uncorroded by self-indulgent nostalgia, idealist fantasies, or a disabling cynicism. All these express a class attitude, summed up in 'Mothers and Sons' as 'something between shame and the pride of the convalescent in his tyrant bed'. But the narrator of the essay can see a cure: convalescence implies a transition to health, a movement which is enacted by the narrative structure of the essay itself.

Only in the recovery of that verbal sincerity and wholeness, that sensuous immediacy of vision and speech which characterized less self-conscious ages, can the poet escape the impasse in which Thomas saw his predecessors transfixed. The successful poet, he argues in an early review in *The Week's Survey*, achieves an effect at once 'strangely mystical and strangely material', in which fact is transfigured into symbol quite naturally (so that in 'Lob', the Hog's Back *is* the Hog's Back). And this 'extreme definiteness of imagination', he says, in a passage which connects his literary theory with the social populism that pervades his writings, 'is a link between the peasants and the greatest poets, who constantly prove that they have seen what they have imagined' (13 December 1902).

V

If We Could See All:
Thomas and the War

Thomas's enlistment may in retrospect seem inevitable, but it should not be forgotten that for several months he had been toying with the quite alternative possibility of emigrating to America to join his son and Robert Frost. The war was not for Thomas the invigorating challenge it seemed to such young men as Rupert Brooke. But it did fulfil his wish for some complete break with 'things as they are'. Thomas's populism, like that of Jefferies, had always fused a radical commitment to 'the people' with 'a large and not always latent power of conservatism . . . as [of] the land itself'. In a period of popular discontent and pre-revolutionary agitation such a credo seemed unambiguous. But in a phase of general reaction such uncritical commitment easily assumed a quite different form.

Trade union membership between 1910 and 1914 had risen from 2,565,000 to 4,145,000; 'the Parliamentary Labour Party could only watch impotently as the use of blacklegs several times led to bitter clashes between troops and strikers', writes David Kynaston in *King Labour* (p. 162). At the Labour Party Conference in 1911 Keir Hardie had proposed strike action in the event of war; in August 1914 the Independent Labour Party declared that 'across the roar of the guns, we send sympathy and greetings to the German Socialists' (Robert E. Dowse, *Left in the Centre*, 1966, p. 20); and Ramsay MacDonald, opposing the war in public, prophesied in private that 'in three months there will be bread riots, and we shall come in' (Peter Stansky, *The Left and War*, 1969, p.61). Paul Thompson writes that 'it seemed possible that, but for the outbreak of war, the autumn of 1914 might have brought a decisive battle' between capital and labour, and 'a general strike in 1914, moreover, might have drawn uncomfortable inspiration from the Irish crisis' (*The Edwardians*, p. 256). J. H. Thomas, the railwaymen's leader, threatened the House of Commons with his union's money being 'used to provide arms and ammunition' on the Ulster model (*The Times*, 25 March 1914). Even after the outbreak of war, Thompson continues,

> There were moments when industrial unrest became very widespread and even a political strike against the war seemed possible. But as before the war, the revolutionary strike never in fact materialized. The war, while heightening tensions, also ... interrupted for at least two years the pre-war momentum of general industrial conflict. It removed a high proportion of active younger workers to the armed forces. Above all it meant that any widespread industrial unrest was vulnerable to its own success, for the military danger which it would cause. When faced by angry crowds of wounded soldiers, the engineering rank and file were not prepared to force a decisive strike against the war. Only defeat in the war itself could have produced a really revolutionary situation. (p. 258)

It was to such working men, from land and city alike, that Thomas directed his attention and admiration in his reporting of nationwide reactions to the war, in such essays as 'England', 'Tipperary' and 'It's a Long, Long Way'. These essays confirm how rapidly the mood of the pre-war period turned, not into the jingoism of the popular press and the fat patriots, but into a quiet and almost melancholy determination to see it through, though he does in 'Tipperary' record the resentment against bosses and state at the widespread dismissal of younger unmarried men to drive them to enlist.

The war, whatever its causes, reactivated the central, conservative impulse of English culture, and suppressed overnight that developing radical consciousness which, given time, might have matured into a more adequate critique of British institutions. The clarion that sounds in 'The Trumpet' calls men to 'rise up' to an 'earth new-born'. The poem ironically echoes 'The Message of the March Wind' and the socialist anthem, 'England arise, the long, long night is over'. But this new earth and new heaven is not that of a millenial dawn. Instead we are invited to 'Forget, men, everything/On this earth new-born' at the very moment that we are told to 'Open your eyes to the air'. This forgetting is a crucial act. For the trumpet summons, like Lord Kitchener's pointing finger 'Up with the light, / to the old wars; / Arise, arise!'

The echo of Morris's closing line, 'And tomorrow's uprising to deeds shall be sweet', co-opts its socialist exuberance to the cause of a dying England. Thomas had called that poem 'a noble piece of humanity', in which the breach in being between public and private experience had been 'healed in a union between love of one woman and of the world'. In 'The sun used to shine' he attempted the same healing through the mediation of the war, which also takes up individual lives into a transcending totality:

> The sun used to shine while we two walked
> Slowly together, paused and started
> Again, and sometimes mused, sometimes talked
> As either pleased, and cheerfully parted
>
> Each night. We never disagreed
> Which gate to rest on. The to be

> And the late past we gave small heed.
> We turned from men or poetry
>
> To rumours of the war remote
> Only till both stood disinclined
> For aught but the yellow flavorous coat
> Of an apple wasps had undermined;
>
> Or a sentry of dark betonies . . .

Here the metaphors ('undermined', 'sentry') connect
to the constantly intruding rumours of war, just as
later the 'pale purple' of the crocuses suggest 'sunless
Hades' fields' (and the implicit contrast with *their* sun).
Nevertheless, history here seems to have been arrested,
all time compounded into this instant of happiness, so
that, for once, 'The to be/And the late past' seem to
have no power, and even this threshold moment,
paused at a gate, seems not to issue into any threatening future, or emerge from any regretted past. The
moon's rising is then syntactically correlated with the
thought of those remote strangers with whom it is
shared:

> The war
> Came back to mind with the moonrise
> Which soldiers in the east afar
> Beheld then. Nevertheless, our eyes
>
> Could as well imagine the Crusades
> Or Caesar's battles . . .

If, previously, time had been compacted into this
moment of pause, it is now stretched out, so that what
is contemporary but remote in space also becomes
remote in time. At the same time, in imagination, all
wars from Caesar to the present seem to share a single,
discontinuous time apparently insulated from their
immediacy. History is initially seen as something

beyond and unconnected with personal experience, as if these walks were somehow outside time, so that the movement out from the personal encounter to the universal relation is temporarily arrested. Yet the individual time scale is only arbitrarily bracketed off from that larger chronology. The poem has maintained a constant present tense until this point. The apparently timeless moment it recalls is now passed away. What presides over the past tense of the poem is that moon whose rise added a retrospective coldness to those remembered scenes, and also surreptitiously reminded of their ephemerality. Those scenes are now remembered, in the present tense, by a poet who is himself at the front. He has become one of those previously remote 'soldiers in the east afar', and now it is the walks themselves which recede to 'faintness like those rumours'. Yet in this very deprivation lies a movement out into a deeper sense of solidarity. Other men now walk those fields and think of him and his fellows at the front, just as he and Robert Frost once did. He knows now, in the phrase he cites from Traherne, that he is 'concerned in all the world' (*SC*, p. 138), that he has never been outside history. The gaps between Caesar's campaigns, the Crusades, and the present war are no more, for the mind which knows only the vanishing present, than the brief pause at the line ending between 'The to be / And the late past', or the passage between the sun shining at the opening of the poem, the moonrise halfway through, and that infinite succession of future moonrises which the poem affirms, in closing:

> Everything
> To faintness like those rumours fades –
> Like the brook's water glittering

Under the moonlight – like those walks
Now – like us two that took them, and
The fallen apples, all the talks
And silences – like memory's sand

When the tide covers it late or soon,
And other men through other flowers
In those fields under the same moon
Go talking and have easy hours.

The tide and the shore, under the moon, awaken faint
rumours of the apocalyptic anger in *The South Country*:
'It was intolerable that they were not known to me,
that I was not known to them, that we should go on like
the waves of the sea, obeying whatever moon it is that
sends us thundering on the unscalable shores of night
and day'; but they are very faint, and there is no trace
here of the indignation or the thunder. Instead, there is
a calm, almost elegiac acceptance, as if, finally, that
gap in mutual knowledge had been overcome, as all
eyes focus on the one object that half the globe can view
simultaneously, and which men and women have looked
at since time began. An idea of England has, it seems,
closed the gap between these separated subjects, effect-
ing that change he wrote of in the essay 'England':

> England then as now was a place of innumerable holes and
> corners, and most men loved – or at any rate could not do
> without – some one or two of these, and loved all England
> but probably seldom said so, because without it the part
> could not exist. The common man was like a maggot snug
> in the core of an apple; without apples there were no cores
> he knew well, nor apples without cores. (*LS*, p. 102)

Yet the image of the maggot complicates that of the
wasp in this poem. For if this 'commonwealth' of
England is undermined, it is by its own 'common men'.
In that discrepancy between innumerable parts and an

[190]

ungraspable whole lurks still the possibility of a larger dispossession, which can only be resolved metonymically, by focusing all those acts of cognition upon the one object they share – that moon which is nevertheless, in the English poetic tradition, a symbol of the unattainable, a cold and aloof object of desire, as for that warrior-poet who also died in Flanders, Sir Philip Sidney, who seems to be remembered here ('With how sad steps, O Moon, thou climbst the skies!'). The gaps remain, like those silences which intersperse conversation, momentarily redeemed from meaninglessness by shared affection. Though in this complex interchange of awarenesses all are bound together by a community of language that sets a seal on a shared humanity, what really links them is their common deprivation and the transience of lives as easily erased as traces on the sand. Everything, including the most intense experiences of solidarity and affection, fades to faintness like those rumours. Experience remains as fluid as the brook's water under the moon, in that favourite image of Thomas's derived ultimately from Shelley, but also here calling up a passage from Wordsworth on 'a bygone patriotism defeated in its own land . . . the patriotism of the Ancient Britons' which Thomas quotes in 'England':

> Mark, how all things swerve
> From their known course, or vanish like a dream;
> Another language spreads from coast to coast;
> Only perchance some melancholy Stream
> And some indignant Hills old names preserve,
> When laws, and creeds, and people all are lost.

In 'Digging', which draws for its list of battles on Thomas's 1915 *Life of the Duke of Marlborough*, these 'Ancient Britons' are themselves called up in fantasy to set his own preoccupations in context. The unbearable lightness of being is matched by the lightness of a represented 'immortality' which is similarly no more than a matter of traces. Here, too, time is compacted, but now ironically in those strata of earth which contain all that is left of millenia of deeds in 'the living air'. The pun on 'matter' is something which puts the whimsical subject in his place, for, like the pipes, he too is little more than clay, as he acknowledges in this act which confuses traces, upsetting the record, by burying together pipes smoked by men two hundred years apart, one already dead, the other aware of his mortality:

> What matter makes my spade for tears or mirth,
> Letting down two clay pipes into the earth?
> The one I smoked, the other a soldier
> Of Blenheim, Ramillies, and Malplaquet
> Perhaps. The dead man's immortality
> Lies represented lightly with my own,
> A yard or two nearer the living air
> Than bones of ancients who, amazed to see
> Almighty God erect the mastodon,
> Once laughed, or wept, in this same light of day.

Again, there is a shared light and earth; but the latter is itself composed of the remains of those who once shared them. The deliberate shift from archaeological time to that of a Creation myth indicates just how much 'immortality' is a matter of 'representations', of imagined, fabular totalities, just as the poet himself begins by imagining some future response to unearthing his pipes, and ends by imagining some primal moment of laughter and weeping, closing off past and future in the brief present of the poem by this cyclical return of language – a sleight of tongue, perhaps, which adds a tinge of ambiguity to that 'Lies . . . lightly'.

'England', 'Britain', that is, remain, not a matter of actual places, but of the stories we spin out of them, the ideological cocoon in which we wrap ourselves. It is possible to see the faintest echo of the 'maggot' metaphor in the suppressed spider of that passage in which Thomas tries to define how England can be a real place when it is really a congeries of subjective experiences, spun out of our own entrails:

> I believe that England means something like this to most of us; that all ideas are developed, spun out, from such a centre into something large or infinite, solid or aery, according to each man's nature and capacity; that England is a system of vast circumferences circling round the minute neighbouring points of home. (*LS*, p. 111)

Perhaps the most consummate expression of such a vision is the poem 'As the team's head-brass'. The opening sentence of the poem correlates two otherwise unrelated events: 'As the team's head-brass flashed out on the turn/ The lovers disappeared into the wood.' On the turn of the line, as of the plough, the lovers disappear – at the beginning of the poem walk out of it as if for good. The casual perception is placed at once as that of an actual man in a real world – so involved in it that had the horses not turned at precisely that point he would have been trodden down by them:

> I sat among the boughs of the fallen elm
> That strewed the angle of the fallow, and
> Watched the plough narrowing a yellow square
> Of charlock. Every time the horses turned
> Instead of treading me down, the ploughman leaned
> Upon the handles to say or ask a word,
> About the weather, next about the war.

The lovers' disappearance has already set up the possibility of other points of view upon a common world, but we are confined to the poet's perspective. The war, too, exists beyond the poem's edges, and the exchange of questions and answers, in its spasmodic, interrupted quality, already hints at those gaps between various centres which are to become the poem's dominant theme. Two men from different classes, poet and labourer, are brought together accidentally by a fallen elm. Before the poem finishes, this convergence is to assume the force of a destiny.

The contrasted leisure and labour of the two presents, in miniature, a profound social gap, and a gap which breeds the growing guilt of the poet. That casual 'Instead of treading me down' quietly introduces the whole question of choice and necessity at the poem's heart. The equally quiet correlation of war and weather raises the same question. The loose, unstructured present, it appears, has a history; it is like this because other things happened or did not happen. The very fact that he is sitting where he is is evidence of this, for the tree stump would already have been moved but for the war:

> The blizzard felled the elm whose crest
> I sat in, by a woodpecker's round hole,
> The ploughman said. 'When will they take it away?'
> 'When the war's over.' So the talk began –
> One minute and an interval of ten,
> A minute more and the same interval.

The whole poem is full of such disjunctions, whether in the conversation of the two men, or the disruption of work patterns caused by the blizzard, which comes to seem a natural precedent for that larger dislocation effected by the war – a dislocation which has its consequences even at the microcosmic level, since the tree's fall interrupts the customary rhythms, and cannot be made good until the war is over. The conver-

[194]

sation shifts, disjunctively, apparently away from the elm, to the problem of personal commitment:

> 'Have you been out?' 'No.' 'And don't want to perhaps?'
> 'If I could only come back again, I should.
> I could spare an arm. I shouldn't want to lose
> A leg. If I should lose my head, why, so,
> I should want nothing more . . . Have many gone
> From here?'

The repeated *I*'s stress a self-absorption in the poet at odds with the self-effacing sense of community of the labourer. The poet's ambiguously subjunctive reply (possibility hovering on the edge of obligation – 'should', 'could', 'ought') is short-circuited by the conditional 'If I could'. Reservations of this kind are not in fact possible. Truly to make the commitment would require free acceptance of all the listed options. The war, the unpredictable blizzard, demands sacrifices, alerts them to the danger and reality of choice. Touched on a sore spot, the poet shifts the conversation away, only, in a dramatic peripety, to come face to face once more with his obligations:

> 'Yes.' 'Many lost?' 'Yes, a good few.
> Only two teams work on the farm this year.
> One of my mates is dead. The second day
> In France they killed him. It was back in March,
> The very night of the blizzard, too. Now if
> He had stayed here we should have moved the tree.'

That strategically placed 'if' pauses before the totality of commitment, in bitter parody of the poet's own conditionals. It now stands revealed. If his mate had stayed, not only his life but the whole world would have been different. Though blizzard and battle are again linked as agencies of an inhuman destiny, the fall of the tree and the fall of the man are distinct. The tree succumbed to irresistible natural forces. The man chose to put himself in a position where death was possible or even likely. A whirl of alternative presents swims before the eyes. The poem itself pivots on this man's conditioned absence:

> 'And I should not have sat here. Everything
> Would have been different. For it would have been
> Another world.' 'Ay, and a better, though
> If we could see all all might seem good.'

The lines divide the syntax perfectly in a mimesis of the tragedy: 'Everything' (as in 'The sun used to shine'), split off from the past and now impossible subjunctives concentrated in that middle line, which then spills over to the lost, impossible world that, retrospectively, we can posit as the product of a different choice. The labourer's speculative, momentary rebellion against the fact of death sinks back at once into fatalism and acquiescence. He is too modest to aspire to godlike omniscience. Unlike Hardy, but like Thomas, he accepts the constraints of a limited human perspective.

The poet too learns a lesson in humility. One cannot impose conditions. He cannot step back from the flux to assess, like some President of the Immortals, the chances and the opportunities. It is at this point, as if to underscore the moral, that the lovers reappear, in a final interruption of the narrative which also, as in 'Digging', brings it full circle. In the passage of time between beginning and end, other lives have been involved in other kinds of converse beyond the poem's borders, beyond the closed conversation of poet and ploughman, and now bring it to an end:

> Then
> The lovers came out of the wood again:
> The horses started and for the last time
> I watched the clods crumble and topple over
> After the ploughshare and the stumbling team.

At opposite ends of a shared landscape, the lovers seem remote from the concerns of the two men. Yet the class relation is quietly linked to the sexual one, through that image of the crumbling clods in which future growth is assured by present disturbance. Work reciprocally reproduces human and natural orders, but so does love-making, and the two together balance the threatening associations with men who also 'crumble and topple over' in battle. The enemy are no different from the lovers at the other end of the field; only distance, and a different point of view, divides them. 'If we could see all' we might see that this catastrophe is only one more expression of 'the one energy that propagates and slays' of which Thomas wrote in *Richard Jefferies* (pp. 300–1), a necessary prelude to rebirth.

The prospect of that rebirth is latent in the poem. The poet turns away to move on, a sadder and a wiser man. But the dialogue of two strangers has deepened into a stronger bond of solidarity, of which the vehicle and symbolic host is the memory of the lost mate. This solidarity has in turn radiated outwards to encompass many others within its circumference: the men gone from and those who remain on the farm, the men at the front, the lovers whose act may have brought another life into existence to balance the absent dead at the poem's centre. The poem's language has enacted this transformation, shifting from the detached third person singular of the ploughman, through the reciprocal relation of 'I, you, me' which, in conversation, reaches out again to a third person, in which the ploughman becomes 'I', his mate 'him' and finally both together another 'we'. And that private 'we' then changes, in the recollection of the collective totality which contains their special views, into a corporate 'we' which involves the whole world: 'If we could see all'. What the war seems to have established is a community of suffering in which it is possible for men to talk to each other again, on common ground, despite all divisions of class and culture.

This is a fine poem, and part of its quality lies in its refusal to round off so easily to such patriotic closure. For, even at the level of the pronouns, a disturbing counter-current runs below the surface, embodied in that third person plural 'they' whose referent shifts, unnoticed, from the poet's query 'When will they take it away?' to the ploughman's 'The second day/In France they killed him.' For the impersonal 'they' to whom the poet refers, in his abstraction from this community, is immediately given tangible first person presence by the ploughman: this 'they' is *us*. But the alien 'they' of the ploughman's speech is the Germans, enemies who remain excluded from the community of discourse. And as long as that division persists, that repeated 'all' at the centre of the text will ride roughshod over the human subjects who try to see and control it.

In the essay 'This England' which is the prose source of 'The sun used to shine', Thomas speaks of that moment of recognition in which he decided to enlist:

At one stroke, I thought, like many other people, what things that same new moon sees eastwards about the Meuse in France . . . I was deluged, in a second stroke, by another thought, or something that overpowered thought. All I can tell is, it seemed to me that either I had never loved England, or I had loved it foolishly, aesthetically, like a slave, not having realized that it was not mine unless I were willing and prepared to die rather than leave it as Belgian women and old men and children had left their country. Something I had omitted. Something, I felt, had to be done before I could look again composedly at English landscape, at the elms and poplars about the houses, at the purple-headed wood-betony . . . who stood sentinel among the grasses or bracken by hedge-side or wood's-edge. What he stood sentinel for I did not know, any more than what I had got to do. (*LS*, p. 221)

The perplexity is like that in 'Old Man': he seems to be listening, lying in wait, for a significance he should yet never can remember. His actual disaffiliation intensifies the guilty anxiety that he must do something, justify his foolishness and incompetence. Yet both external and internal worlds are a puzzle to him, as that last sentence reveals: knowledge founders in an excess, a 'deluge', of suggestion, but this is not thought but 'something that overpowered thought'.

Tragically, the war became, for a generation of superfluous men, the supreme experience that could vindicate their absurd and redundant existences. It represented a spiritual commonwealth which offered shelter from the anomie of history. The war became more than a mere defence of something they already had. It became, instead, the process by which they could acquire that from which they had always been excluded. It seemed to offer a liberation from the dead shell of an alienated order which, in the pre-war world, had cancelled out or confiscated those momentary intuitions of an older and more authentic way of life, where significance was real and immediately apprehended.

One might have to go a long way back before 'England' was anything but a name, but the essay 'England' gave it away with its remark: 'A writer in *The Times* on patriotic poetry said a good thing lately: "There may be pleasanter places; there is no *word* like home." . . . We feel it in war-time or coming from abroad, though we may be far from home: the whole land is suddenly home' (*LS*, p. 108). And yet this atavistic impulse is revealed for the delusion it is in that poem called, not 'Home', but '"Home"', stressing that it is the

[199]

word, and not the reality, to which its three superfluous men respond. In the poem, the landscape through which they travel is, in a familiar contrast, both fair and 'strange', and the snow casts out 'all that was/Not wild and rustic and old'. Yet there is a tangible 'nothing' at the heart of this landscape, as of this journey, too, for 'There was nothing to return for, except need' – a necessity which remains unexplained throughout the poem. The words of one of them at sight of the cold roofs where they must spend the night are ironic indeed:

> 'How quick,' to someone's lip
> The words came, 'will the beaten horse run home'
>
> The word 'home' raised a smile in us all three,
> And one repeated it, smiling just so
> That all knew what he meant and none would say.
> Between three counties far apart that lay
> We were divided and looked strangely each
> At the other, and we knew we were not friends
> But fellows in a union that ends
> With the necessity for it, as it ought.

This is the only moment of speech in the whole poem, and it is significantly not dialogue but exclamation. Each man has his own separate response, and the word is a mere abstract focus for their different losses and defeats, with no concrete content of its own, an empty signifier. 'Home', that is, defines a lack – that 'nowhere' where each of these modern men actually lives. 'England' is here dispersed into an evaporating set of absences, the negative side of that overlapping system of circumferences spoken of in the essay of that name. Throughout the poem, none of these individuals is given any concrete identity: they are simply 'someone', 'one', 'all', 'each' and 'other', 'none'. Each in fact is the 'no man' who inhabits this No Man's Land. This is

why the disparity between knowing, meaning and saying grows, deepening rather than closing the gulfs
between them. If the landscape is 'strange', so too, are
the men who 'look strangely each/At the other', in a
complex web of negative reciprocities. In the process,
'need', a personal and subjective thing for each, is
translated into a tyrannous objective 'necessity', a
necessity which by the end of the poem has taken on
the quality of a Babylonian captivity, in which the self
is forever exiled from its authentic being.

In the crisis of significance where words and
speech, thought and thinking, look, meaning and
emotion fall apart, the self almost evaporates, unable
to fix itself in the circuits of a shared language that
might guarantee the integrity of each. Thus the *word*
'home' suggests the *word* 'homesick', for to accept anything more than an empty counter would be to admit
too much. 'Admit' here means not only speak, but also
give way and allow entry to, almost, too, a confession of
guilt, as if the captivity were a justified sentence. To
survive, he cannot admit the real feeling, but must
perpetually keep it at an estranging distance, sealed
off in the play of signifiers. The desperate revolt in that
'Must' is therefore undercut at once by the futile ineffi-
cacious 'somehow', which shares in the vagueness of a
self who is, or seems to be 'Another man', and whose
very life is threatened with being no more than 'an evil
dream':

> Never a word was spoken, not a thought
> Was thought, of what the look meant with the word
> 'Home' as we walked and watched the sunset blurred.
> And then to me the word, only the word,
> 'Homesick,' as it were playfully occurred:
> No more. If I should ever more admit
> Than the mere word I could not endure it
> For a day longer: this captivity

[201]

Must somehow come to an end, else I should be
Another man, as often now I seem,
Or this life be only an evil dream.

There is no explicit reference to the war, but the 'cold
roofs' are those of Hare Hall military training camp,
where the poem was written in March 1916, as his
letters to Frost, Bottomley and Farjeon reveal. (He had
written to her in February, 'Somebody said something
about homesickness the other day. It is a disease one
can suppress but not do without under these conditions' – *LFY*, p. 188.) The war has brought no real
change, no access of 'community'.

'This is no case of petty right or wrong' has to be read
in the light of this realization. It accounts for much of its
sense of absurdity, not only in its disdain for 'fat
patriots', 'politicians or philosophers' and those who
'grow hot/With love of Englishmen, to please newspapers', but at a deeper level. The Kaiser cannot be
hated because he is a ludicrous figure: 'A kind of god he
is, banging a gong', but then, the whole world of public
discourse, in both camps, shares this absurdity. It is not
a question of choosing between either Kaiser or fat
patriot, or even between justice and injustice. Yet, if it is
not a question of rational judgements about rational
rights and wrongs, what is it about? Thomas's response
is uncharacteristically evasive. He is 'Dinned / With
war and argument' and, his intellect thus dulled, he can
'read no more / Than in the storm smoking along the
wind / Athwart the wood'. Repeatedly, of course, storm,
mist, an intimidating nature, have been used as figures
of destiny in Thomas's writings. But here the natural
metaphor does not hold, but shifts at once into a supernatural one which, at the same time, indicates the
human origins of that ideological magic in which he is
ensnared:

> Two witches' cauldrons roar.
> From one the weather shall rise clear and gay;
> Out of the other an England beautiful
> And like her mother that died yesterday.

These witches are out of *Macbeth*, and the spell they weave is one which traps the prevaricating self into bloody ambitions and, finally, his doom. Yet what is obvious here is the poet's recognition of the trap into which he has fallen. If he is 'Dinned/With war and argument' he also deliberately *chooses* to 'read no more' – refuses, that is, the dispassionate interpretation of events which might free him from them. He has not quite succumbed to the mood which he described in the article called 'War Poetry' in December 1914: 'The demand is for the crude, for what everybody is saying or thinking or is ready to begin saying or thinking . . . [The public] want something raw and solid, or vague and lofty or sentimental.' But the poem is closer to this than to the 'settled mystic patriotism which war could not disturb' which he found in Blake. Disturbance is everywhere in this poem, in fact. It is there, for example, in the self-deprecating evasion dressed up as bravado in the next lines:

> Little I know or care if, being dull,
> I shall miss something that historians
> Can rake out of the ashes when perchance
> The phoenix broods serene above their ken.

No phoenix, of course, ever rose from a witches' cauldron. Thomas already here acknowledges his doubts, even in that unconvincing dismissal of history's rational gaze. He is not good at obfuscation, and the rising rhetorial crescendo of the closing lines only compounds the sense of a discriminating mind trying to dull itself into commonplace. Even the echoes of

John o'Gaunt's deathbed speech, the origin of the phrase 'this England', subvert the rhetorical intention, for Gaunt dies, we should recall, lamenting an England 'now leased out . . . /Like to a tenement or pelting farm', which has 'made a shameful conquest of itself'. Knowledge, in the closing sentence, has turned into blind 'trust', an instinctive 'lived' faith that substitutes for real perception, and a circling logic steels him to the hatred he feels he *should* experience:

> She is all we know and live by, and we trust
> She is good and must endure, loving her so:
> And as we love ourselves we hate her foe.

The stridency here does not obscure the infiltrating doubts. The poem distrusts its own brash assertions, exonerating itself by pleading extenuating circumstances. The freedom affirmed here is not a possession, but a set of relationships between people to be reborn, like the phoenix, in a communal solidarity. But the 'we' of a collective identity is forced, its prerogatives not to be relied upon: does it, for example, include the fat patriot? The tightrope act falters; the discriminating voice joins the din.

History, for Thomas, is constantly conceived of in terms of two powerful but contradictory metaphors which sharpen the contrast between reified institution and living process. On the one hand, history is a house within which the individual life occurs; on the other hand, it is a perpetual flux, an endless stream in which the self is swept along. In 'The Long Small Room' it is both the oddly shaped house and the leaves streaming in the wind; in 'Two Houses' the haunted house and the flashing river. 'Gone, gone again' starts with the second metaphor, but then moves out from exposure to the estranging flux into a wider perspective. It is a poem which should be read whole, since so much of its

presentation of history depends upon the careful
cadencing of its narrative rhythm:

> Gone, gone again,
> May, June, July,
> And August gone,
> Again gone by,
>
> Not memorable
> Save that I saw them go,
> As past the empty quays
> The rivers flow.
>
> And now again,
> In the harvest rain,
> The Blenheim oranges
> Fall grubby from the trees
>
> As when I was young —
> And when the lost one was here —
> And when the war began
> To turn young men to dung.
>
> Look at the old house,
> Outmoded, dignified,
> Dark and untenanted,
> With grass growing instead
>
> Of the footsteps of life,
> The friendliness, the strife;
> In its beds have lain
> Youth, love, age and pain:
>
> I am something like that;
> Only I am not dead,
> Still breathing and interested
> In the house that is not dark:—
>
> I am something like that:
> Not one pane to reflect the sun,
> For the schoolboys to throw at —
> They have broken every one.

Written at the beginning of September 1916, the poem records the second anniversary of the outbreak of war in August 1914. The powerless self looks on at the stream of history. But this is the imaginary detachment of the aesthete, like that Oscar Wilde he censured in a review for writing 'a literature of the idle classes, for the idle, by the idle. Life flows past it, while it languidly watches the waves; only now and then there is a cry, and a watcher has fallen in and gone down; and still life flows past, regardless of the voice repeating "Experience, the name we give to our mistakes"' (*DC*, 13 June 1908). The note of personal loss acts as a dramatic reminder of how unreal is this separation, for the 'lost one' is seen to be the displaced focus, the absent centre where personal and historic meanings converge. The loss occurs at their intersection. The apples ironically call up one of those battles fought by Marlborough. But there are other resonances. Each man sits at the centre of his private little England, like the maggot in the core of an apple. The very grubbiness of the ambiguous epithet prevents any easy assurance about rebirth. If the personal death is seen now to be part of a natural process in which destruction is the necessary prelude to renewal, the word 'dung' nevertheless carries its full weight of disgust. There is no individual transfiguration. The tragedy is inexpungable. But the very inhuman extremity of the war is, of necessity, the end of one civilization, and the seedbed of another.

The poem moves inexorably from the personal grief to the larger crisis. The house is virtually derelict, with an irrelevant, bankrupt dignity. This is, finally, what happens to that manor house celebrated so equivocally in *The South Country*, emptied of its significances. The war seems, almost, the only redemption of human society, without which it would rot in its own inertia.

[206]

After the cataclysm, life can never be the same again. The helplessness and isolation of the speaker make him, like the house, dark and untenanted. He too has been emptied of his meanings. He remains, now, simply a moment of attendance, a mere openness to the unknown future. The war must destroy the old order completely, drain it of its last nostalgic resonances, before any progress can be made.

This is, of course, the significance of the apples which fall already grubby from the trees. The corruption is there already in lives undermined by a decaying civilization. His yearning for the future is fused with his longing for the past. The old house is cut off, scorned by the future generations, who see its dereliction. A war capable of destroying civilization is trivialized to the image of schoolboys throwing stones at abandoned windows in a way which adds to the plangency. Here perhaps, in these final lines, lies the whole pathos of the superfluous man. In the yearning for something beyond the dilapidated present, he learns his own inability to identify with 'the house that is not dark'. His roots are too deep in the past. Yet he sees too that in the dead, outmoded edifice lies the cause of his estrangement and futility. The only remedy seems to be a sacrifice of the self that belongs to this order, choosing that war that turns young men to dung. He is not dead, but the way to the future lies through his death. The old house can only redeem itself through a sacrifice which affirms the possiblility of the new house, the new society.

That Thomas should see his death as part of the conflagration from which the phoenix might rise explains, perhaps, the tenacity, the integrity of his commitment. The broken windows let in the fresh air; are, perhaps, the windows of another poem, which he wished to see broken. That poem had spoken of a whole

[207]

society confined in its class-divided solitudes, where the neighbourly thing would be to swallow one's pride and cast the first stone. But it is still *others* who have to take the initiative, as in the cry, in *The South Country*, 'Where was he who could lead the storming-party?'

'I built myself a house of glass' represents the negative side of that 'system of vast circumferences circling round the minute neighbouring points of home'. In *The Happy-Go-Lucky Morgans* in 1913 he had given a similar negative variation upon the image in explaining the superfluous man:

> The magic circle drawn around us all at birth surrounds these in such a way that it will never overlap, far less become concentric with the circles of any other in the whirling multitudes. The circle is a high wall guarded as if it were a Paradise, not a Hell . . . or it is no more than a shell border round the garden of a child. (p. 49 ff)

The Country, published in the same year, extended the metaphor, in a wishful attempt to resolve the dilemma of the superfluous man by reducing him to that 'nothing' which repeatedly for Thomas lies at the heart of England and self alike. Community can be found, he suggests, by seeking those moments of lonely exaltation for which we have seen an explanation in William James. We go to the country:

> to escape ourselves, and we do more than escape them. So vastly do we increase the circle of which we are the centre that we become as nothing. The larger the circle the less seems our distance from other men each at his separate centre; and at last that distance is nothing at all in the mighty circle and all have but one circumference. And thus we truly find ourselves. Many cannot bear this expanding circle, this devouring silence, and they seek another kind of nearness by crowding to Eastbourne or the Bay of Naples. (p. 55)

Or, one might add – in sorrow, not anger – to the fields of France.

For Thomas, the chosen death was a humane sacrifice, not suicide. Seeing the dereliction of his own age and self, he needed to affirm a different reality, a new house in which friendship and strife, youth, love, age, pain, and the whole activity of men and women, could once again have meaning. Significance, for Thomas, in the end arises from solidarity. And that means a choice of directions, and of those with whom one travels.

'Roads' is a poem which takes up and generalizes a metaphor which often in his writings seems a symbol of mere individual vagrancy. But here, roads assume their full, social meaning, as the historic routes by which we define and endow with meaning our own 'private' journeys. The pilgrimage to be 'at home in the world' is here seen to be a public quest:

> I love roads . . .
>
> Roads go on
> While we forget, and are
> Forgotten like a star
> That shoots and is gone.
>
> On this earth 'tis sure
> We men have not made
> Anything that doth fade
> So soon, so long endure.

The individual subject is always an illusory construct, like 'the traveller/Who is now but a dream only', his own dream, or the dream figment of his own society. Evanescent, ghostlike, he haunts a material world he has created and which lives beyond him, in an endless succession of passing mortals. Endurance, indeed, is the key concept in these poems of Thomas's: a going-on, when shorn of all purpose, in the tenuous hope

that some meaning will finally be disclosed. For, in the
end, all the passing ephemeral events of history are
only moments of that deeper momentum discerned by
the old woman in 'Mothers and Sons': 'the froth made
by the deep tide of men's inexpressible perverse
desires'. In the figure 'Helen of the roads' the personal
and the historic merge; for the social spirit of the lonely
roads, the embodied meaning of the journey, is the
poet's wife who is also the Celtic goddess, archetype of
all endurance and fruitfulness and survival, giving
significance even to the empty house:

> Helen of the roads,
> The mountain ways of Wales
> And the Mabinogion tales
> Is one of the true gods,
>
> Abiding in the trees,
>
>   . . .
>
> And beneath the rafter
> Else uninhabited
> Excepting by the dead;
> And it is her laughter
>
> At morn and night I hear
> When the thrush cock sings
> Bright irrelevant things,
> And when the chanticleer
>
> Calls back to their own night
> Troops that make loneliness
> With their light footsteps' press
> As Helen's own are light.
>
> Now all roads lead to France
> And heavy is the tread
> Of the living; but the dead
> Returning lightly dance.

'Now all roads lead to France.' In reality, yes. But in Thomas's poem they also lead in the opposite direction, back to their own night, for the returning dead. Seeking that night, the poem leads us in a different direction, to the mountain ways of Wales, but also into a mythical dimension where alone those ways can be truly recovered, just as the roads earlier wind into the night 'On the mountains of sleep', possibly to reveal Heaven at the next turn, or conceal Hell in the next pine clump. It is only, that is, in the order of fantasy that contraries can be reconciled, and the divided subject unified in an unproblematic Englishness.

This remarkable double movement goes to the heart of Thomas's dilemma, his allegiance looking Janus-faced at every threshold in opposite directions, to France, to Wales, to the old and new houses, to the past and the future. This is why 'the dead/Returning lightly dance', freed at last from an impossible historical dilemma. Only posthumously can such men as himself return to the uninhabited rafters of their culture. It is, significantly, the apparently accidental image of the house inhabited only by ghosts which seems to prompt the quickening of tone.

Even here, then, the superfluous man still inhabits a twilight realm, still travels on wondering where he shall journey, O where? The poem ends on a similar perplexity, salvaged only by the feeling that, at last, he has allowed something else to make his choices for him. The antitheses persist to the end. The undirected noise of the towns seems as 'irrelevant' as that of the birds, for it is multitude without association. The returning dead, on the contrary, crowd out his solitude, by speaking of a common purpose in which alone lies liberation and community. Flight at last can be reconciled with responsibility. Solidarity can be found in sacrifice. Clearly, for Thomas too, the road led inevitably to France. The English ideology which I have tried to unravel in this book sealed off certain options, made certain 'choices' inevitable, rounded certain 'accidents' into a fate. In the last stanzas of the poem the traveller is still waiting upon those 'accidents', still he seems unsure of what will happen next, defining his whole life in terms of a patient attendance upon external events. But this is only on the surface. For he knows already that he has come 'home', has found his place among the company of the dead, where alone the posthumous, the superfluous man can find his significance. Now –

> Whatever the road bring
> To me or take from me,
> They keep me company
> With their pattering,
>
> Crowding the solitude
> Of the loops over the downs,
> Hushing the roar of towns
> And their brief multitude.

In 'England' in 1914 Thomas had written: 'If England lies like a vast estate calm around you, and you a minor, you may find faults without end. If England seems threatened you feel that in losing her you would lose yourself.' In 'This England' he was prepared to countenance that loss, realizing, he said, that 'either I had never loved England, or I had loved it foolishly, aesthetically, like a slave', and 'that it was not mine unless I were willing and prepared to die rather than leave it.' At 7.36 on the morning of Easter Monday, 9 April 1917, a stray shell falling on Beaurains Observation Post added another name to the roll-call of illustrious corpses who have died for that idea. By the end of this war to end all wars, nearly one in every ten

[212]

British men under the age of forty-five had joined that list. The dead and wounded numbered over two million.

Truly, 'This England' is a costly business.

Bibliography

The initials after some books below are the abbreviations used throughout the text. In addition, *DC = Daily Chronicle* and *MP = Morning Post*.

Principal prose works by Edward Thomas

The Woodland Life, 1897
Horae Solitariae, 1902
Oxford, 1903
Rose Acre Papers, 1904
Beautiful Wales, 1905
The Heart of England, 1906 [*HE*]
Richard Jefferies, 1909 [*RJ*]
The Hills and the Vales, by Richard Jefferies, introd. by
   Thomas, 1909
The South Country, 1909 [*SC*; page numbers throughout my
   text refer to the Everyman reprint, 1932]
Rest and Unrest, 1910
Feminine Influence on the Poets, 1910
Windsor Castle, 1910
Rose Acre Papers, 1910
Light and Twilight, 1911
Maurice Maeterlinck, 1911 [*MM*]
The Isle of Wight, 1911
George Borrow, 1912
Lafcadio Hearn, 1912
Algernon Charles Swinburne, 1912
The Icknield Way, 1913
The Country, 1913
The Happy-Go-Lucky Morgans, 1913

Walter Pater, 1913
In Pursuit of Spring, 1914
Four-and-Twenty Blackbirds, 1915
The Life of the Duke of Marlborough, 1915
Keats, 1916
A Literary Pilgrim in England, 1917
Cloud Castle, 1922
The Last Sheaf, 1928 [*LS*]
The Childhood of Edward Thomas, 1938
Letters from Edward Thomas to Gordon Bottomley, edited
    and introduced by R. George Thomas, London, 1968 [*LGB*]
*A Language Not To Be Betrayed: Selected Prose of Edward
    Thomas*, selected and introduced by Edna Longley,
    Manchester, 1981

Main editions of the poetry

Collected Poems, with an introduction by Walter de la Mare,
    10th edition, London 1969
Poems and Last Poems, edited by Edna Longley, with a
    substantial selection of prose source material, 1973 [*PLP*]
The Collected Poems of Edward Thomas, edited by R. George
    Thomas, the variorum text of the poetry, Oxford, 1978
For the most part, the text used in this Student Guide is
taken from the Faber edition, but on occasion the variorum
text has been preferred.

Biography and criticism

Barker, Jonathan (ed.), *The Art of Edward Thomas*, Cardiff,
    1986
Cooke, William, *Edward Thomas: A Critical Biography*,
    London, 1970
Coombes, Henry, *Edward Thomas: A Critical Study*, London,
    1956
Eckert, Robert P., *Edward Thomas: A Biography and
    Bibliography*, London, 1937
Farjeon, Eleanor, *Edward Thomas: The Last Four Years*,
    London, 1958 [*LYF*]

Harding, D. W., 'A Note on Nostalgia', in *Scrutiny*, vol. 1, no. 1, May 1932.

Leavis, F. R., *New Bearings in English Poetry*, London, 1932

Marsh, Jan, *Edward Thomas: A Poet for his Country*, London, 1978

Moore, John, *The Life and Letters of Edward Thomas*, London, 1939

Motion, Andrew, *The Poetry of Edward Thomas*, London, 1980

Poetry Wales, Edward Thomas Centenary Issue, vol. 13, no 4 (Spring, 1978)

Scannell, Vernon, *Edward Thomas*, British Council Series, London, 1962

Smith, Stan, 'A Public House and not a Hermitage', in *Inviolable Voice: History and Twentieth-Century Poetry*, Dublin, 1982

Thomas, Helen, *As It Was* and *World Without End*, London, 1956

Thomas, R. George, *Edward Thomas*, Aberystwyth, 1972

Thomas, R. George, *Edward Thomas: A Portrait*, Oxford, 1985

Index

[219]